apathy and other small victories

Paul Neilan

apathy and other small victories

ST. MARTIN'S GRIFFIN   NEW YORK

www.stmartins.com

Library of Congress Cataloging-in-Publication Data

Neilan, Paul.
      Apathy and other small victories / Paul Neilan.
            p. cm.
      ISBN-13: 978-0-312-35219-6
      ISBN-10: 0-312-35219-0
      I. Title.

      PS3614.E443 A88 2006
      813'.6—dc22

                                                2005044804

10 9 8 7 6 5 4 3

To my parents, who will hopefully never read this book

Acknowledgments

Huge thanks to the following people:

My mother and father, for always giving me the support and the space to do my own thing, even when they weren't really sure what that thing was.

My brothers, for all thinking the same weird stuff is funny, and for all speaking the same movies.

Simon Lipskar, for doing all the things people say you can't expect an agent to anymore, from the initial revisions all the way up to that big phone call, and for staying involved and excited about everything that's come since.

Ben Sevier, for making it a better book and funnier, for walking me through the whole editing process, and for asking the hard questions about very small animals.

Dan Lazar and everyone at Writers House, and Jenness Crawford and everyone at St. Martin's Press.

Siobhan Dooling, Paul Forti, Neil Gupta, Jack Hamlin, Jason Pagano, Anthony Papariello, Jessica Swenson, and everyone else that I've stolen from over the years.

And special thanks to Carrie Moore, for giving it the first read and a better ending.

 part one

Chapter 1

I was stealing saltshakers again. Ten, sometimes twelve a night, shoving them in my pockets, hiding them up my sleeves, smuggling them out of bars and diners and anywhere else I could find them. In the morning, wherever I woke up, I was always covered in salt. I was cured meat. I had become beef jerky. Even as a small, small child, I knew it would one day come to this.

That Sunday I could feel my head pounding even before I opened my eyes. I might have kept them shut all day if there hadn't been two men standing over my bed.

"All right partyboy, time to get up," one of them said in a gruff, weary voice.

I blinked a few times. I was very confused. I didn't know who either of them were, or what the fuck they were doing in my apartment. They both had their shirts tucked in and the older one, the one with the gruff voice, had a low hairline that started just above his eyebrows and a drooping mustache that hung along his sagging jowls. He looked like a walrus. The younger one had slicked-back hair and squared shoulders and perfect posture. He was smirking like he couldn't wait to show me how cocky he was. He looked like every cop that had ever given me a ticket.

"Smells like criminal intent in here," he said, glaring at me.

"What?" I said.

"I was gonna ask you the same thing," he said, challenging me in a way that I did not understand.

The older guy looked annoyed at both of us.

"I'm Detective Brooks," he said, "and this is Detective Sikes. We're here to ask you a few questions."

"Don't you need a warrant or something? How did you get in here?" I couldn't think of anything I'd done that would get me arrested. If stealing a few saltshakers was wrong I didn't want to be right.

"Your door was wide open so we came in, just to make sure you were okay. And we don't need a warrant to ask you a couple of questions. We just want to talk."

"Oh." I had my bedsheet pulled up to my chin and I was clenching it with both fists for some reason. It must have been the goddamn vampires again.

"Why don't you sit up like a big boy and talk to us," Sikes said.

"No thanks, I'm very comfortable."

"Where are your manners," he said, smirking. "Rise and shine fancy pants!" and he grabbed the bottom of my sheet and yanked it away from me like my father used to do with my blanky when I was very small, but this time I didn't cry. And I knew that I was finally a man.

I was still wearing my shoes and the same clothes I'd been

fired in on Friday, except now everything was covered in salt. There was a pile of it on my bed, and I was buried underneath it like the sleeping dad on the beach who wakes up to find that his mischievous asshole children have played a joke on him with their buckets of sand and their cruelty. But these men were not my children, and there were no saltshakers anywhere. Where had it all come from? How had this happened? I had no idea. I have never been able to explain myself.

"Bling bling. Looks like somebody had themselves a little fiesta," Sikes said. "What've we got here, coke? H? Mexican chimmy hat?" He stuck his pinky into his mouth and then dipped it in the salt. "You're going away for a long time señor," he said as he jammed his salt-speckled finger up his nostril.

"Sergeant that doesn't look like—" Brooks started to say, but Sikes was already snorting. His eyes watered and he started coughing and sneezing in short fast fits like a dog. He blew his nose into his hands and rushed to the bathroom, slamming the door behind him. The faucet was on for a long time and he was coughing and spitting and crying.

Brooks looked at me strange.

"You sleep in salt?" he said.

"Sometimes."

"Good for your back?"

"It's all right."

"You famous or something?"

"Not really," I said.

He considered the possibilities, then decided I was guilty of some undetermined perversion and shook his head. We both listened as Detective Sikes heaved into my sink. I wished the guy in the apartment above me would start fucking his guinea pig again, just to give us something else to listen to, but he did not. Those kinds of wishes almost never come true.

When the cocky prick finally came out of the bathroom his face was raw and smeared, his eyes puffy from all the crying. He looked like a burn victim, one who'd been through numerous successful surgeries but still wasn't fully healed. It's tough to ever really recover after your face has been on fire. I stared at him pretty fucking bemused but he wouldn't look at me.

"Now that you've cracked the case," I said, smiling at Sikes and his chafed red nose, "I really would like to get back to sleep. I bid you both good morning."

"It's two in the afternoon," Brooks said.

"No shit."

"Like I said, we have a few questions for you."

"All right," I said, and sighed.

I was still foggy and my head was throbbing, but I could play vice squad with these two for a few minutes. It would make them feel like they were being useful, and it would be an interesting start to my day. I just hoped I hadn't done anything stupid the night before. I didn't remember anything illegal. I didn't remember anything really.

"Where were you last night, around 10 P.M.?"

"Probably at a bar."

"Probably?"

"Probably."

"What bar?"

"The one down the street."

"What's the name of it?"

"What's this about?"

"How well do you know Marlene Burton?"

"Who?"

"The assistant at Dr. Weinhardt's office. Your dentist."

"Oh, deaf Marlene."

"She had a last name." Sikes broke his shame-induced silence. "She wasn't defined by her disability. She was a person too you know."

I know, fuckhead, I signed in response, working my hands slow for emphasis. I waited for him to react. I wanted to slap away the cockiness that was already creeping back into his blotchy, running face. When it was clear that he had no idea I'd called him a fuckhead in sign language I said, "What about her?"

"Marlene Burton was found dead last night."

My dentist's name was Dr. Weinhardt but I called him Doug. Doug had episodes. He'd flip out and have to lie down and monitor his pulse and breathe slow and in rhythm like a pregnant woman or else he'd faint, which he usually did anyway. He thought iced tea helped, so he kept a pitcher of it in his back office on a table beside his fainting couch, and he carried a monogrammed flask with him wherever he went. The monogram was D.W.I. Douglas Weinhardt the First.

"But D.W.I. are the initials for Driving While Intoxicated! And it's a flask but there's no alcohol, it's only iced tea. Get it? And I don't even drive! I take the bus every day! That's funny, right?"

"Jesus Doug."

He thought his episodes were being caused by a series of brutal attacks he'd suffered recently. This is how he explained it to me:

"About three months ago I was getting off a bus downtown

when all of a sudden—Psshew!" He smacked both his hands against his ears. "The big folding accordion door closed right on my head! And then there must have been a malfunction or something because it just went Wham! Wham! Wham!" He pressed the air around both sides of his head three times fast with his palms, spreading his fingers and holding his elbows high, like some New Wave dance that was so embarrassing no one even joked about it anymore. "It kept slamming into my head until I fell out into the street. When I woke up there was a crowd of people standing around me and a man was snapping his fingers in my face. The bus driver said he'd never seen anything like it. I couldn't stand up without falling down again. I had to ride home in the back of an ambulance. And then a few weeks later, on a different bus with a different driver, it happened again! It's happened six more times since. I don't even call the ambulance anymore. I just crawl around until my equilibrium comes back."

"Christ Doug. Maybe you should see a doctor."

"I am a doctor," he said.

It would have sounded smug if he hadn't just finished telling a story about getting his head jackhammered by a bus door. It's real hard to come off as even slightly superior when you're living a *Tom and Jerry* episode.

Doug had a dental assistant named Marlene. My first appointment I was reclined in the chair and Doug was gouging my teeth and gums with something he called the *sharpo*. "Just cleaning the plaque out of the gutters," he said as blood drained into the back of my throat.

There was a bright light hovering above me like the ones

aliens and angels use to trick people into not running away and I was breathing hard through my nose and panicking because I was choking to death on my own blood. Then I heard someone else come into the room, their shoes softly padding the floor. The light steps sounded like a woman's.

"Oh there she is. Just in time. Can you hand me the pro-ber?" Doug said.

He was speaking very slowly and louder than a normal person should. A woman's hand passed between me and the light. I saw red nails, and I was very impressed with myself. I had always been perceptive. I could've been a detective. I could've been blind and still been able to solve crimes and mysteries. I was almost like a superhero sometimes.

"No no, the pr-o-ber," he said way too deliberately, adding an unnecessary syllable. I figured she was either six years old or retarded. If she was that young she shouldn't be wearing nail polish. And if she was retarded she'd better not be allowed to play with the drills.

"Thank you. Now can I get some suc-tion? Suc-tion?"

She put the thin vacuum tube in my mouth and it sucked and slurped the blood from the back of my throat as Doug kept hacking away. I could breathe again. This woman had saved my life. I would probably marry her, even if she was six years old and retarded. We would have a strange life together.

"Oh gosh, you two haven't even met! If someone's putting their hands in your mouth you should at least know their name," Doug said. "Shane, this is my assistant, Marlene."

A head leaned over close to me, eclipsing the tricky, paranormal light. There was a serene halo of blond hair lit up all around her face. Single strands hung down like icicles. It was beautiful.

"HI NICE TO MEET YOU!" she shouted atonally into my gaping mouth.

I saw this documentary once that had black and white footage of a man in goggles and baggy clothes. He looked vaguely German, or like someone the Germans would've taken prisoner back when everything was black and white. He was pale and skinny and his head was shaved bald. His legs were in stiff, clunky iron boots and his arms were shackled and pulled straight down at his sides by taut chains bolted to the floor. He looked very nervous.

Then shit started flying all over the place. He was standing in a wind tunnel. The force of the wind blew his baggy shirt and pants tight against his skinny body and the fabric flapped and rippled behind him frantically as his arms shook in the shackles, but the iron ski boots kept him from blowing away. The goggles protected his eyes but his mouth was wide open and his lips were pulled back exposing his teeth like a horse on one of those hillbilly postcards. He looked like he was screaming but the only sound was the whir of turbines and the rushing wind. That's where the footage ended, but I'm pretty sure his head got blown off soon after. I think it was some kind of experiment.

And that's how I felt. Like a vaguely German prisoner in leg irons and chains whose scream could not be heard above the deaf girl wailing in my face. Soon my head would be gone too.

Later, as Marlene was putting away the sharpo and the prober and humming loud and off-key to herself, Doug leaned towards me and said, "She's deaf you know." But he said it under his breath, discreetly, so she wouldn't hear.

I spit more blood into the sink.

* * *

Doug spent most of his time freaking out in his back office, so that's how I got to know deaf Marlene.

I'd never actually talked to a deaf person before but I'd been swimming and gotten water stuck in my ears lots of times, felt that underwater silence as I shook my head and watched people's mouths moving without hearing the words, so I knew what it was like for her. I could empathize. And I always used to watch reruns of *The Facts of Life* when I came home from school and I had vivid, uncomfortable memories of those episodes where Blair's stand up comedian cousin would mock herself to get laughs and teach tolerance to Mrs. Garrett and the rest of the girls. She had cerebral palsy but she talked like a deaf person, so the lesson was the same. I could sympathize, and pity.

"Hey so how long have you worked in this place?" I said.

She was standing right next to me looking at a dental chart, and of course she couldn't hear a goddamn word I was saying. I barely resisted the impulse to clap or snap my fingers.

"Hey So How Long Have You Worked In This Place?" I said again, because sometimes it is hard to remember not to be an ass.

Marlene glanced up in mid-sentence and saw that my mouth was moving, and when it stopped she smiled and nodded her head and laughed quietly and politely, just like hearing people do when they don't know what the fuck you just said. Blair's cousin was right. We are all the same.

We stared at each other and it was so awkward I considered murdering myself or giving her the finger just for something to do, but instead I made a fist and stuck out my thumb and screwed it into my cheek. I saw a monkey do it on *Sesame Street* once. It means *apple* in sign language.

"APPLE! LIKE THE MONKEY!" she shouted, genuinely excited. Deaf girls love *Sesame Street*. We both laughed for as long as we could, which was for much longer than it was funny.

She had too many teeth going in different directions. Her hair was a frizzy mess, like she was three weeks past a bad perm, and the blond dye kit was obviously cheap and self-applied. But still, she pretty much looked like anybody else. She didn't look especially deaf. But she was. She was.

There was the kind of silence you can only have when it's high noon, or when one of you is deaf.

I pointed at her, then pinched my nose closed.

She narrowed her eyes, confused, then shouted, "I'M NOT STINK!"

And we laughed about that for a long time.

When the detective told me she was dead there was a pause in my head where I thought of absolutely nothing, a hitch where nothing happened, just before the engine caught. When it did I wanted to make myself scream "No!" and start crying, but I knew that I couldn't, even under the circumstances, and that fact had a better chance of bringing me to tears than Marlene's death. I almost said "No shit," which would have been my natural reaction, but this was no time for natural reactions.

"Jesus," I said quietly, and lowered my head like I was thinking, which I was.

"We'd like you to come down to the station, answer a couple of questions," Brooks said.

"Why me?"

"It's nothing personal, we're talking to everybody she had any contact with. Just gathering information."

"Why can't you just ask me here? Why do we have to go down to the station?"

"We also need a sample."

"A sample?"

"Semen was found on the body."

"Eww."

"What, you don't like semen?" Sikes said, challenging me again.

"All right, you want to do this the easy way?" Brooks broke in. "Come on down to the station."

"Am I being arrested?"

"No, we're just going to ask you a few questions."

"Do I need a lawyer?"

"That depends."

The trick is to be like Robinson Crusoe. Wherever you find yourself shipwrecked you build a temporary home out of palm leaves and sticks. You use hollowed out coconuts for lemonade glasses or to make string bikinis that you will never ever wear. You use sand and water. You make mud for no reason. Whatever's lying around, you use it. But the trick is you build everything so flimsy that it has to fall apart. And when it does it looks like an accident, like unfortunate circumstances, or bad luck or timing. And that's your way out. Then you go get shipwrecked somewhere else and start building again. Wash, rinse, repeat. Why these are the tricks, I do not know.

*   *   *

I would've gotten out long before Marlene was murdered if it hadn't been for Gwen. I couldn't just walk away after knowing Gwen. Literally. I was incapacitated. Sometimes for days at a time. But it was more than that. Gwen was what hysterics think of marijuana. She led to crack and giving handjobs for a dollar on the street. Or their moral equivalents at least.

I fought my way out of her ghetto—I got thrown out actually—but I was stuck there just long enough that I fell right into a bigger, much worse pile of shit when I left. I suppose I could blame myself for how it turned out, but I've never been comfortable with that sort of thing.

It was before I'd started stealing saltshakers. I'd just gotten into town so I didn't know anything yet. I was alone in a trendy bar that had overpriced drinks and a doorman who'd called me "Boss" when he asked for my ID, then said, "Thanks guy" when he gave it back. I had the hiccups pretty bad. I had to keep my sentences short so people wouldn't think I was epileptic. This made everything I said sound very wise.

"Hi, I'm Gwendolyn," she said, standing beside me at the bar. She had a round face and straight hair down to her square shoulders. I had been drinking scotch to impress any strangers who might have been watching me, and I was so drunk I could only see geometry.

"Hello Gwendolyn," I said in the quiet time between hiccups.

"Please, call me Gwen. Only my grandmother calls me Gwendolyn."

Then why the fuck did you introduce yourself as Gwendolyn, I wanted to ask, but that was way too many words in a row.

"Yeah," I said instead.

Gwen worked at a big insurance company where she made important decisions. She was very decisive, but she would've liked the opportunity to be even more so.

"It's hard sometimes because things can be so structured, and it feels like seniority gets rewarded over how much work you actually put in. I don't want to disrupt the dynamic of the team—we all work so well together—but then I don't want to get pigeonholed and wind up stuck in the same position two years from now either."

"Labels are terrible things," I said.

"That's so true."

We were connecting.

Then we were on the front steps of her apartment and she was bashing the inside of my mouth with her tongue. My dental work was crumbling like the moon does in movies when it's the end of the world.

"Maybe we shouldn't," she said, and pulled back. Before I could agree she was mauling me again.

"Mmm, I don't know," and she pressed the side of her head against mine like we were about to Greco-Roman wrestle.

"I also don't know," I said, but then both of her hands were on the back of my head and she was stuffing me in her mouth like that little Japanese guy who eats all the hot dogs. It is a strange sensation, being devoured.

"This could be trouble," she said.

She was right. If not for her brute strength propping me up I would've gone headfirst down the concrete steps and broken my beautiful face on the sidewalk. Then she had me pinned up against the wall. It felt glorious to lean. Far, far below me, the ground spun.

"This isn't a good idea," she said.

"There are no good ideas anymore," I said, and then a hiccup rocked my entire body and rolled my head like I'd been shot. "Just be happy we thought of something."

I think it's a line from an old John Cusack movie. If it's not then it should be.

I shouldn't have said it. That's obvious now, and it probably was then too. But I really didn't have a choice. I needed to either lie down or throw up, and to do one or probably both on her front steps would have been tacky. And I had to go to the bathroom. And I really had nothing else to do that night anyway. In my scotch-soaked estimation, spending the night with a deceptively powerful stranger didn't seem like such a bad idea. I had already mistakenly kneed her in the crotch when we first started making out, so I knew she wasn't a man. That seemed like enough of an endorsement. And I'd always wanted to play a John Cusack role. For a line or two at least.

One line was all she needed. She kicked the door open and flung me inside. I fell over something and broke my ankle, but the alcohol made the swelling seem funny.

And that was it for me. My already tattered memory was done. Thank you and good night.

When I woke up the next morning the room reeked of latex and chlorine.

Oops.

My ankle wasn't broken but it hurt real bad, and so did my head. My whole body hurt really, and I didn't know why. I didn't remember getting hit by a truck or beaten with a lead pipe.

She had to go to work but she said she'd give me a ride home.

"Where did you say you worked again?" she said after we'd ridden in silence for a long, long minute.

"I just moved here. I don't have a job yet," I said.

The already awkward scene turned full-blown excruciating. Her face went red as she focused on the road and kept her hands in a rigid 10-and-2 grip on the wheel, and I turned on the radio to keep from opening the door and throwing myself out of the car. At twenty-five maybe, but she was already going thirty and still accelerating. I would've gotten all messed up.

A commercial said the circus was coming to town, so to ease the shame and the silence I pretended to be afraid of clowns. Everybody's afraid of clowns, so I thought maybe that could be something intimate between us that we could share forever, like the drunken sex I didn't remember from the night before. I of course wasn't afraid of clowns, but I figured she had some story about getting kidnapped at a circus or sodomized at a rodeo or something. Anything. And sure enough, a rodeo clown had fucked her in the ass when she was seven years old. Actually it was more like, "I've always been afraid of Ronald McDonald. I think it's all the makeup." It was harrowing in its own way.

My story was about how they had big shoes and noses but drove such little cars.

"It's more a fear of incongruity than clowns I suppose."

The conversation was riveting.

"Right up here's good," I said.

We were fourteen blocks from my apartment but I had nothing left. The inanity and the awkwardness was just too much to bear.

"Hey thanks for the ride."

"You're welcome," she said. "I gave you my number, right?"

"Yeah," I said.

But she was waiting for something else. The silence that followed was unmistakably uncomfortable, almost crippling. She was waiting for some kind of decision, some explanation. Or at least a hint.

I looked at her and tried to think of what I could possibly say next. Her eyelashes were stubby and not long enough to curl. This made her eyes look bigger than they actually were. She did have a round face, but she really wasn't as sharply geometrical as she'd seemed the night before. I could see why I'd thought so though. And still my head was empty.

Her right hand twitched on the steering wheel and I had the panicked thought that she might try to put the car in PARK, so I grabbed the door handle and jumped the fuck out. "Thanks again," I said, leaning in before I slammed the door. And I waved to her as I went up the steps of an apartment building that was not my own.

She pulled away slowly, and as she drove off I threw up all over someone's front door.

I have always been vaguely and uselessly talented. I can hop on one foot longer than anyone I have ever met. For the period from 1983 to 1991 I can name every player and their position just by looking at the picture on the front of their baseball card. I can

do cartwheels even though I've had no formal gymnastic train-
ing. I can touch my tongue to the tip of my nose and lick my nos-
trils. I can hug myself so tightly that from behind it looks like
someone is slow dancing with me. I did it at my senior prom and
when I inched my hands down my back to grab my own ass the
assistant principal said he'd send me home if I didn't stop "being weird." No one ever had to teach me how to drive a stick
shift. Somehow I just knew. My fourth-grade teacher said I had
the finest penmanship she'd ever seen from a boy. She urged me
to take up calligraphy, but I did not. Still, the beatings on the
playground were savage. I can whistle, I can juggle, and if I'm
drunk enough I can and will wrap both my legs behind my head
and play my ass like bongos. I would have dominated the Renaissance. But I was born much later, so instead I was sitting in
Doug's dentist chair sketching deaf Marlene.

I'd started bringing a bag whenever I went in for an appointment. Magazines, music, pornography, a sketchbook, a journal,
some snacks. It was like the bag my mother used to bring to
church for me when I was little, full of toys and distractions so I
wouldn't start crying and interrupt mass and piss off the priest.
Because if I did, he'd tell God to make us die in a car crash on
the way home.

"Can't we just wear our seat belts?"

"Seat belts are no match for God," said my mother.

I played with my GI Joe figures and learned how to be quiet
and afraid.

Marlene stood by the window with her hands on her hips, her
jaw set like a Roman emperor. I had her lift her chin so the light
caught her badly dyed hair and made it shimmer like wet, dirty
straw. She was a fascinating subject. I could've spent hours on

her straw hair alone. It was much more than a bad perm I realized. It looked like a vitamin deficiency. Maybe she was using the wrong shampoo.

After a half hour I was done. I signed my name, perfectly legible but with an elaborate renaissance flourish, and handed her the portrait.

Voilà.

"HEY! THAT'S NOT ME!" she shouted.

I'd drawn her head huge, a caricature with horse teeth and Alfred E. Newman ears and pockmarked dimples on her basketball-sized cheeks. Her eyes were bulging and had two *X*'s instead of pupils, like she was drunk or had just been hit over the head with a mallet, and her tongue was hanging out. Her tiny body was squeezed into a string bikini, her legs crossed at the ankles, and she was sitting on a pile of garbage. Squiggly stench lines rose all around her like shitty apparitions. Her hair looked nice though. My art was not true but I was a good person, and kind.

Asshole! Why didn't you draw me right? she signed.

Yes, I signed. My vocabulary was not big.

Why?

I am genius.

You're an asshole!

GENIUS!! I signed again.

To say *genius* in sign language you hold your thumb and forefinger like you're measuring an inch on each hand, then you put one against your forehead and hold the other about six inches away and jiggle both slightly for emphasis. The way I did it I looked like I was having a migraine seizure on a cable car during a catastrophic earthquake. My whole body shook and my inch-measuring hands flailed and slammed against my forehead and flew around like I was in a rapture or getting riddled with bullets. Sign language is very dramatic. It's like being in a silent movie. Sometimes you have to overact and look ridiculous just to get your point across.

Why didn't you draw me good, weirdo? She was laughing at my genius.

Because you stink.

"I'M NOT STINK!" she shouted. *And I don't have big ears!*

No. You have a tiny head.

Shut up! she signed, but she still took the picture.

On the ride downtown the two detectives explained that while I was certainly entitled to have a lawyer present during my questioning, it would be easier on everyone and much quicker if I waived my right to counsel. If I hadn't done anything wrong I really wouldn't need a lawyer, would I? And since I didn't seem like the kind of guy who had his own attorney on retainer that would be a few hundred dollars I'd have to shell out just to get someone to sit there and hold my hand. Did I really need someone to hold my hand while I talked to the big bad detectives? Maybe I needed someone to hold my dick for me while I pissed too. And maybe they knew a few guys in lockup who'd be happy to do it for me. How about that?

I could have a lawyer provided for me of course, but that would take time, and those lawyers were young and overworked and they weren't any good anyway. Why would I want to make things difficult for everybody? Life was hard enough without intentionally making it harder on yourself, wasn't it?

To anyone who'd ever watched cop shows on TV the insinuation was obvious. I knew what they were suggesting. So I decided to forgo legal representation, just as I decided to forgo being sodomized with a splintered baton in a backroom of the station later that night.

They left me sitting alone in a small room with a long table. I was on one side, three empty chairs were on the other. There was a tinted rectangular window by the door and the light overhead was a few shades brighter than it should have been. This was where they would break me.

I had decided to mostly tell the truth. I had almost nothing to hide. Not about Marlene being dead anyway. But I still didn't know what was going on and what part they thought I had in it, and I didn't want to give away too much before I did. They didn't know that I didn't know anything, and I was hoping to use that to my advantage. The only thing I had going for me was my ignorance. This was the story of my life.

Chapter 2

The next time I saw Gwen after throwing up on that stranger's door, it was a little awkward.

We had to go through the usual small talk motions of getting to know each other after the fact, and I learned many interesting things about her, like how she loved to talk about her job and always ended her laugh with a "hah hah, hmmm" sigh before moving on to the next topic, which was usually her job. I also learned that she had a slightly crooked nose that she'd busted playing rugby in college. It was just a little off, but in a way that once you noticed made her face immediately more interesting and less attractive.

She didn't learn anything about me, but she got the chance to ask all the basic questions she figured she should've asked before sleeping with me in the first place. I was subtly evasive and vague and made mediocre jokes and changed the subject back to harmless neutral topics like herself. That's all anyone really wants to talk about anyway.

She didn't want answers. She just wanted to ask for them.

Nobody really likes definitions in those situations, even if they pretend or think that they do. In the long term everyone traffics in foregone conclusions, and in the short term they just get drunk. This is the way it has always been. Some half-assed ambiguity masquerading as mystery is all anybody's really looking for. That's why transvestites are always in such a good mood.

And there we were, two transvestites in our platinum wigs and heels, sitting in a bar, stirring our drinks, stumbling through the drag show that is life. We talked about how cold it was getting.

"Unseasonably so," I said between hiccups.

Again, we were connecting.

Later, back at her apartment, I found out why I was so destroyed after our last night together.

I have never been overly aggressive or forceful with women. I'm not that guy who throws her on the kitchen table and rips open her blouse, popping all the buttons and ruining a perfectly good shirt. Or who fucks her up against the wall in a dark alley behind some Dumpster. I never wanted to be Mickey Rourke. I don't think he did either. It takes a willful suspension of absurdity to be that kind of man, to maintain that five o'clock shadow, to buy that leather jacket, to put all that shit in your hair, to keep that toothpick in your mouth when all you really want to do is spit it out and buy a pack of grape Bubblicious and go watch cartoons.

Still, when it comes to sex there's always been the tacit understanding, or the pretense of the tacit understanding at least, that I'm in charge. That even if I'm not the guy in the back alley behind the Dumpster, I'm at least some guy. A guy at least.

Not with Gwen. She manhandled me.

It was always a blur of pain and fear and domination. I remembered it, and could only deal with it afterwards, as a collection of warped Polaroids stapled to the inside of my head:

Me flat on my back, my arms splayed out like I was being crucified, my legs kicking helplessly with her on top leaning over, crushing my biceps with her hands and screaming in my face.

Me on top of her, my back arched, my mouth wide open, my head almost snapping off at the neck because she was pulling my hair, while her other hand palmed my side with almost hydraulic pressure, collapsing my lung and squashing my spleen.

Me behind her but backed into the ornate wooden headboard of her bed, frantically trying to push her away as she slammed me against the wall with her ass.

Me on my back again, both my arms pinned above my head, her one hand vise-gripping both my wrists, her other hand flat on my chest, her fingers popping my ribs like bubble wrap.

Whatever position we were in, I was the one getting fucked. At first I tried exerting myself, gently, but firm enough to let her know that I could take over any time I wanted to. But then I felt the raw power, the machine-like force and resistance. It was unyielding. I would've had to push full out and strain with everything I had to overpower her, and even then I wasn't sure that I could. I didn't want to find out that I couldn't.

Not that she was a big girl or anything. She was about 5'7", medium frame, built like any twenty-five-year-old woman who keeps in shape. But she was fucking solid, and thick, without being broad or outwardly mannish. Her muscles must have been coiled tighter than a normal person's. Maybe they were more dense. There was something mutant about her. Because I don't go around getting out-muscled by girls. Not usually anyway. But with her there was nothing I could do. She was the sadistic older brother who holds you down and slaps your forehead over and over again, lets a string of spit fall until it almost hits your face and then slurps it up, over and over again. Only this older brother was fucking me. I'm telling mom.

I tried faking an orgasm but she either didn't notice or didn't care. I tried bucking her off but that only made it hurt worse. My bones were weak from the pounding. My pelvis was shattered. My whole body felt like early onset osteoporosis. I'd have to join a swimming pool therapy class and lift a beach ball over my head with the rest of the old ladies at the Y. Is calcium more potent if you snort it? I was brittle. I was a broken man.

And then, after it was over, after she was done kicking my naked ass until there was nothing left of it, she had the audacity to curl up on my dislocated shoulder, nestle her head underneath my fractured jaw and sigh and say, "Hold me. Hold me tighter."

"I can't. My arm is broken in three places."

"Ahh, that feels so good. To know you're there. It feels so safe."

This as I was openly weeping.

I lacked the strength to be incredulous, indignant, or even

quietly sarcastic. It sounded like some cheap scam straight out of a trashy women's magazine. Some *Please Your Man? Please Yourself!* article on how to use basic psychology and transparent strategy to create the illusion of power in your relationship. There was a cute chess metaphor about queen taking king while leaving all the other pieces on the board, and some anecdotal scientific evidence about how men like to hunt and make fire, how women find shoes and lipstick empowering.

I knew that article. I knew that magazine. And I could tolerate its simple, harmless, vapid philosophy. With enough alcohol I could even participate in it for a few hours at a time. But Gwen was reading a different magazine. One you can only get over the Internet from shadow publishers in former Soviet Republics. One you have delivered to a PO box wrapped in brown paper and sealed in plastic. This article was not called *Please Your Man? Please Yourself!* It was called *He Is Not Boss, He Is Bitch!* And it read in rough translation:

Strip him down. Toss him like rag doll and beat him within inch of life. Beat him until humiliation hurt worse than pain. Maybe set him on fire and laugh. Then be kitten. Tell him he is boss, is brute man, so he will pay for jewelry and fur coats. Pay for trip to America to find old man husband who will die in sleep and leave you rich fortune.

Magazines make me sad.

Some nights, as I lay in bed crying softly with my head under my pillow, I could hear the guy in the apartment above me having sex. I could hear him fucking his guinea pig. The squeals were unmerciful.

He used to take it out for walks on a leash, a long thin chain that was attached to the back of the patent leather corset the guinea pig was always wearing, bulging out of either side like a squashed sausage. It had a cute little leather slave hood strapped over its head so all you could see were its spastically twitching nose and panicked eyes as it scurried frantically all over the sidewalk, straining against the chain, trying desperately to escape. But it could not.

"Hey conchumbo!" its master said, walking towards me as I stood outside the building gasping in horror. I'd heard the squeals a few nights before and convinced myself that it was just the TV, or a warped recording of *The Chipmunks Sing Christmas*. It was the only way I could go on living. But really it was worse than I had imagined.

"You're new to the building right?"

"Yeah," I said, staring first at the guinea pig, then at him. He was at least 6'5" and about 97 lbs, so pale he could've been albino. He had no eyebrows. He was wearing a long leather trench coat that billowed behind him as he walked and a T-shirt with a punk band on the front that I'd never heard of because they weren't the Sex Pistols.

"What apartment you in?" he said in a strange, forced accent, like he'd seen *Scarface* way too many times.

"302."

His leather pants were tight on his spindly legs. There were zippers everywhere.

"That's right below me mambala! Sorry if I kept you up the other night, heh heh," and he smiled and yanked the leash as the guinea pig tried to dart out into the busy street to die.

"I'm Mobo."

"I beg your pardon?"

"My name is Mobo."

"Is that Swedish?"

"No," he said, and looked away. In a far off voice, he continued. "It was given to me by a Honduranian shaman, a man of great power and wisdom." He had a long goatee shaved out away from his face into a nappy stalk that he stroked lightly with his whole hand as he talked. He looked like the pharaoh of a ruined perverted civilization.

"You lived in Honduras?" I said.

"No. The shaman did. I met him one night in an airport in Dallas. I had a layover."

"I see."

"And this bitch here," he yanked on the leash again, "is Ivan."

Ivan darted all over the sidewalk, so close to freedom yet so terribly far away.

"That outfit's . . . something."

"It's waterproof," he said.

"Yikes."

Mobo looked me up and down, still stroking his goatee.

"Listen moncheechee, I know we just met, but I can tell things about people. I have this perception." He cocked his head and listened to the clouds singing as they passed before the sun, but he couldn't hear them because they were too far away. "I can tell you're a man who knows how the game is played."

"Oh jesus."

"What do you say you come up to my apartment and we have a business convo, macho de pucho."

"Uh, I can't. I have to go see my girlfriend. Her name is Gwendolyn." And in that moment, I loved her dearly.

"Ha ha, I know how it is my man. Las minas. Minatas! Ha ha ha." And he laughed at the joke I didn't know he'd made. "That's good. That's good. Stay busy. Keeps you sane. But if you ever need a little something, a little powder, a few pills, you come up to my place. Anytime. You want to get happy, get fucked up, get focused, I'll show you what they *really* put in those piñatas!"

"Uh, what?"

"I sell fireworks too. M-80s, Roman candles, top of the line army issue shit. You get the downstairs neighbor discount."

"That's fantastic."

"There's a lot you can do in this town, a lot that can happen armurro. You just need to know the right people. Come up anytime. Unless you hear me taking care of some *other* business. Then you've got to wait your turn."

And something inside of me died.

Mobo jerked the leash and dragged little Ivan towards the front door.

"Till we meet again mamado," he said, and the door closed behind them.

And they went up to his apartment, the guinea pig stiffening his tiny legs but unable to put up any real resistance. Mobo whispered several Spanish-sounding gibberish words as he dragged the terrified animal into the boudoir. Then he kissed Ivan harshly on his little mouth, and turned off the lights. And many, many laws of God and man were broken in the darkness.

*   *   *

"Ahhh, that was so good."

It was after sex again and my head was broken. I was definitely bleeding internally. I think my brain was injured. I was having trouble doing simple multiplication. That's the test I use to gauge head trauma whenever I'm really drunk or I fall down. I'd never had to do it after sex though. I thought 4×3 was 8, and 7×5 was 200. Fuck.

Gwen and I had been butting heads like rams. She'd lean over and *bang!* smack me right in the forehead, then rear back and do it again. She seemed to like it, but I was real dizzy. I was one of those rams that had no horns, a baby ram or a girl ram, so it was just my soft head getting bashed in. I didn't know what the fuck I was doing on that mountain anyway.

"Ow," I said, lightly running my fingers over my forehead, looking for the crack in my skull. You would think that after so many sex beatings I'd have been numb to the pain, that I was all scar tissue and fused bone and dead inside, but she always found a way to make it hurt like new.

She took a breath like she was about to say something, but then she didn't and I was glad. Then she did anyway.

"At first, I thought you were just using me," she said.

"I definitely am." I just wasn't sure for what.

"Asshole!" she said, and punched me in the side. And she laughed as my kidney began to hemorrhage.

That's the beauty of honesty. Everyone's so unused to hearing it they just assume you're kidding, and you get to feel very good and forthcoming without suffering any consequences except for traces of blood in your urine for the next day or two.

"No," she said, "I was afraid you were just using me to get a *position*," and she waited for me to catch on and chime in with something clever so we could be just like a witty couple on a sitcom. But I was too preoccupied with my internal injuries to play Smothers Brothers. I didn't need laughs. I needed a doctor.

"A *job* I mean," and she grinned, pleased with herself. "But you're not, are you."

"Ugh," I said, and I flinched as she moved towards me, bracing myself for more punishing sex. But she draped her arm over my chest instead.

"Even if you were, I'd help you," she whispered as I slipped into a coma.

"So?" she said, some time later.

"Huh?"

"Do you want me to talk to anybody for you?"

"Huh?"

"Haven't you been listening? At Panopticon. Do you want me to talk to anybody about you maybe getting a job."

"Huh?"

"You'd have to start out on the ground floor, maybe even as a temp. But you'd move up quickly. I know you would."

"What?"

"There's a lot of opportunity," she said, and raised herself up on one elbow. "So do you want me to talk to anyone for you?"

"At your insurance company?" She actually seemed serious. "No thanks, I'm all right."

She looked at me for a long time. Not long enough for me to turn my head and look at her, but still pretty long.

"You're so, *independent*," she said.

It was nice of her to want to believe the best about me. People tend to do that with the strangers they're fucking. If she wanted to think that apathy and independence were the same thing, good for her. Maybe she was right.

And it was nice of her to want to help me out with a job, whatever her real motivations were. Apart from beating the shit out of me during sex she seemed like a nice person. But nice just isn't enough anymore. Everybody's nice, or they at least try to be, or pretend to be. You have to go to France or New York City to find a real asshole these days, and they're only doing it because people expect them to, like those monkeys at the zoo who throw their shit at visitors through the bars. It's more reputation than a real desire to smear feces all over somebody. And that's just sad.

"What are you thinking?" Gwen said.

I pretended to be asleep.

Marlene had been teaching me sign language during those hours when Doug was on the couch in his office, sipping iced tea and sobbing into his hands. She said I was getting pretty good. I knew the whole alphabet and a couple of words, but I mostly said *fuck*, *shit*, *dick head*, *asshole* and *sex*. It was just like first grade.

And just like in first grade, *shit* was my favorite. To make the sign you stick out your thumb and then close your other hand around it, then pull your thumb down out of your fist. It's disturbingly graphic. You can almost hear the *plop*. Marlene said I should be a translator, like at the United Nations, but there's no country where everybody's deaf so I don't know who I could represent. And even if there was a deaf country I doubt me telling the Lebanese ambassador to go fuck himself in sign language would go over too well, geopolitically speaking.

Doug was amazed.

"I can stand here and ask her the same question five times and she has no idea what I'm talking about, but you just move your hands around and she knows exactly what you mean!"

Doug never really understood the concept of sign language. And most of the time I wasn't even signing. I was mashing my hands together and flittering my fingers while clearly mouthing the same question to her that Doug had just asked five times. When he talked he mumbled or played with his mustache or turned his head in mid-sentence. Then he'd say the same thing again, only louder. Doug never understood that for someone to read your lips they need to see your mouth, and that volume doesn't matter when you're deaf. Doug never understood a lot of things.

"I can't believe how quick you picked it up. Did you speak any sign language before you started coming here?"

"No, I did not," I said, while signing *I hate you*.

Marlene barked a laugh, then pressed her lips together as her face went red.

"That's great," Doug said, smiling. "Say something else."

"I speak sign language, but I am not deaf," I said, and signed *I want to throw my shit at you*.

Marlene was trying to strangle the laugh in her throat. She sounded like a gagged hostage whimpering for her life.

"How do you say 'I am a dentist'?" he asked.

I eat my shit, I signed, as Doug haltingly imitated me. Marlene couldn't hold it together. "HMAAA! . . . HMAAA! . . . HMAAA!"

she blared in a series of atonal bursts that rose into strange registers and pitches, then went silent before blaring again, like a malfunctioning boat horn signaling to the shore. She hid her face in her hands.

"Why is she laughing?" Doug asked.

"I'll ask her."

Why do you have sex with my shit? I signed.

Stop it! Asshole! I'm going to get fired!

"She says when we speak sign language it's like we have lisps, and we use broken phrases, like immigrants. She says we talk like lisping immigrants."

"Ha ha, well, we're in the right country for it!" Doug said.

I don't think he even knew what he was talking about.

I eat my shit, Doug signed slowly to her, grinning.

And tears rolled down Marlene's deaf cheeks.

If I could've said for sure where I'd been the night before I would have felt a lot better about sitting in the interrogation room of a police station, but even so I didn't feel that bad. The bright light made the room a little warmer than it should have been, and I was still pretty hung over, but I was getting used to it. I had nothing to worry about. I was probably down at the bar, drinking pitchers of beer and not talking to anyone. I probably was. Everything would be fine.

Detective Sikes walked in holding a manila file folder, his chest puffed out like a little bird. He sat down in the middle chair and laid the folder on the table between us. Brooks was probably at the tinted window with The Chief saying, "Let's see how the kid does."

"Before we get started detective, can I ask you a question?" I said.

"All right." He was immediately thrown off.

"Why did the other detective call you 'Sergeant' at my apartment? I thought detectives and sergeants were different?"

"They are different. Sergeant is my first name," he said.

"Wow. What a crazy coincidence."

"Not really. My dad was a detective. Two of my uncles were cops. My grandfather was chief of police back in the fifties."

"Jesus."

"Yeah. I know," he said, temporarily human and forlorn.

"Detective Sikes, can you come out here for a second?" It was Brooks, talking over a speaker that sounded like it was right above my head. He was pissed.

I tried to keep a straight face as I imagined the shouting that was going on outside. When Sikes came back in his face was flushed and he was all business.

"All right, let's start over. How well did you know Marlene Burton?"

"I knew her all right. I was at the dentist's a lot. Doug has some kind of banged up narcolepsy from getting his head smashed by a bus door, so while he freaked out in his office me and Marlene used to talk. She taught me sign language."

He looked at me the way my mom did the time she caught me officiating the wedding of Mr. Potato Head and He-Man. I had just said, "You may kiss the bride," and when I looked up she was standing in the doorway. I was fourteen years old, and I was not wearing any pants.

"We're in a police station here tough guy. I don't know if you realize how serious this is. A woman is dead." I got the feeling he was trying hard not to have a nervous breakdown, just like my mom did.

"I am being serious," I said.

"When was the last time you saw Marlene Burton?"

"About a month ago, maybe longer. At the office during my last appointment, whenever that was."

"Anything happen between the two of you? She seem like she was okay?"

"Nothing happened. She seemed fine to me."

"You ever been to her house?"

"Nope. Wait once. For a party. She put a sign on my back. It was humiliating."

He looked at me like I had no pants on again. It wasn't my fault. He-Man and Mr. Potato Head were in love.

"Did you have a sexual relationship with Marlene Burton?"

"No way."

"What, you don't like girls?"

"I like girls. She was married."

"Don't like married women huh?"

I immediately remembered my landlord's wife, and I hoped there wasn't more involved in this than I first thought. Things suddenly didn't seem so funny anymore.

·:·:·: Chapter 3

I didn't know what I was doing in that city. I never know what
I'm doing anywhere. I only know how I'll leave. It's always on a
Greyhound. It's almost too easy. They go everywhere cheap and
all you have to do is sit back and look out the window and pretend that motion and direction are the same thing.

The drivers are nice to you as long as you're not obviously
drunk or touching people when it gets dark. Sometimes they're
funny and friendly. They tell jokes like, "Why are Tigger's paws
always dirty . . . because he's always playing with Pooh!" and
"What's the worst part about having sex with a three-year-old
girl . . . the fact that you have to kill her afterwards!" Nobody
laughed at that one but me, and I was mostly being polite.

Sometimes they bark out a list of rules when you get on the
bus and they try to be hard about it because they really wanted
to be a cop or join the army but they couldn't pass the physical
and became morbidly obese bus drivers instead. Sometimes
they say prayers for a safe journey, but it never feels like they're

violating your civil liberties. For the most part they just drive and leave you alone. They're all right. Even that lady who told the joke about the three-year-old. She was just lonely.

It's not the worst way to go once you know what to expect. There's a baby crying on every bus, and a couple is always fighting. Teenage girls are going to visit their boyfriends and teenage boys are going to live with their stepmothers. There's an old woman with huge novelty sunglasses and a pinwheel who won't stop talking to everyone, and somebody's car broke down and they have no other way to get home. There's a pair of nuns up front who don't speak English. Women with creased faces buy one-way tickets and men in camouflage pants eye you up because they think you want to steal their bags. And there's an old man sitting on a bench and looking down at the ground outside every bus station in America.

It's all the people who aren't rich enough for Amtrak or airfare and aren't bothered enough to care how they get to wherever it is they're going. And when they start talking, and they always do, you find that each of them has a story they want to tell. Everyone, no matter how old or young, has some lesson they want to teach. And I sit there and listen and learn all about life from people who have no idea how to live it. Nobody knows how to just shut the fuck up and look out the window anymore.

The bathrooms are tiny and filthy and you have no choice but to piss all over yourself when the bus swerves, but the streetlights look like blurred stars exploding in the window when it rains at night, and you can sleep knowing that if there's an accident and everyone on the bus dies it wasn't your fault. Someone fat and snoring will sometimes sit beside you and sweat on your shoulder even though it's twelve degrees outside, and someone else with a big head shaped like an onion and dirty hair that smells like fish sticks will sit in front of you and recline their seat into your lap. And you'll be trapped and sleepless and sad for the entire ride. But then other times you get two whole seats to yourself, and when that becomes your idea of luxury you know you've found something that no one else is even looking for, and if you gave it to them for Christmas they'd return it the next morning as soon as the stores opened. And then you get to think of yourself like the little drummer boy, playing for Jesus even though he's too young to understand, even though nobody in Bethlehem really likes percussion and they think you're a cheap ass for not bringing gold or frankincense. And it's a shame when you realize that you won't get to be in the Bible, and it doesn't seem right. But then nobody gets to be in the Bible anymore, no matter who they are or what they do, and the sooner you realize that the easier it all becomes. But it's still a shame.

And that's why I had to talk to Bryce. I wasn't going to be in the Bible, so it was time to make other arrangements.

He was crouched low, painting the molding around the front door outside the apartment building. He was the landlord, so he had to do that kind of thing. Bryce was tall, about my height but built, with tattoos twisting all the way up his arms, snakes and hearts and daggers and all kinds of shit. He had a drawn, lean face and the transparent remains of a thinning rockabilly pompadour still clinging to his head. He'd probably been in a band a few years ago, bought into the entire scene, but it hadn't worked out. And now he was stuck with the cigarettes and the sideburns and all those fucking Stray Cats albums. But like the working class hero he'd never become, Bryce hung in the best he could. So while Brian Setzer sang on Gap commercials and pranced around the stage in his fancy pants, Bryce still cuffed his dark jeans and carried his wallet on a chain, still kept the hairstyle even as it betrayed and openly mocked him, still shot pool with a cigarette hanging out of his mouth even though it sometimes fucked up his shot. If it wasn't exactly noble, it wasn't without conviction either.

"So Bryce, we need to talk," I said seriously, but smiling. I was being funny.

"Oh hi Shane. Hi. How are you?"

He stood up from his crouch and held the paintbrush upright so the white paint dripped slowly down the handle and ran onto his tattoos. He didn't even notice. He was too busy scratching the back of his neck and looking at my shoes. He was always much too nervous for a guy with so many tattoos.

"That's just it Bryce." I kept using his name to build trust, like a hostage negotiator. "I'm not so good."

"How much are you short?" His voice cracked on *short* and he dropped the paintbrush.

I was stunned. The element of surprise was gone. I had no more time to build trust and pity. I was the worst hostage negotiator ever.

"Uh, about two hundred."

"Oh . . . Oh . . ." He bent down to pick up the paintbrush but it kept slipping out of his fingers, the handle hopping off the steps with a tedious *tink tink tinktink* that was driving me fucking crazy. I wanted to kick him in the face and run away. Then he stood up without the brush and scratched his neck with both hands.

"We should talk about this," he said. He was even more nervous than usual. He was tearing at his neck and jerking his head around like a frightened animal, looking everywhere except at me. I was about to be evicted. Fuck. This was no good. Obviously I wanted it to happen, but not yet. The timing was all wrong.

"Okay, this is serious," he said.

Goddamnit Bryce, people are supposed to have more faith in each other. Landlords especially. I'm living in your building. That makes you kind of like my dad. Family is supposed to be important. When I stiffed him on next month's rent, then he could throw me out with a clear conscience. Until then he was just being a bad father and a dick.

"This is about my wife," he said.

"I beg your pardon?"

"If you do, I'll take the $200 off your rent."

"Do?"

"Would you?"

Would I what? Did he want me to kill her? In every movie I'd seen that costs more than $200. Was I supposed to have sex with her? That would make me a whore. Did I really want Bryce as my pimp? No, he was paying me, he'd be my john. But what would that make her? She'd be the groom at the bachelor party who fucks the stripper. I'd be the stripper. What?

"I didn't even know you were married," was all I could get out.

"I am." He was ripping up the back of his neck, digging his nails in and tearing it raw. And with the white paint all over his one hand, smearing it around, it was just making me sick.

"I'm not sure what you mean here Bryce."

"I bowl on Tuesdays. Come by then. At seven."

I didn't know he was a bowler. I didn't know a lot of things. He was in the middle of either a complete nervous breakdown or a fucking bipolar episode, I knew that. But he didn't seem grave enough to be suggesting murder, or depraved enough to be asking me to fuck his wife for $200 while he went bowling. He just seemed nervous and real sad.

"Will you? Please?"

The rims of his eyes had gone red. His neck was bleeding and there was that fucking white paint everywhere. His chin was starting to shake. I hate when people show emotion.

"Tuesday? At seven? Uh, sure."

There was a good chance I was going to be murdered. Every scenario I'd imagined ended with me being dead.

If I was there to kill her, she'd suspect it and kill me first: self-defense.

Or I'd kill her, then Bryce would come home and kill me: life insurance.

Or I'd kill her, and Bryce would feel so guilty he'd tell the police everything and kill himself, then the courts would kill me: justice.

If I was just there to have sex with her, she wouldn't know about it and think I was trying to rape her, so she'd kill me: feminism.

Or Bryce would come home, catch me fucking his wife, and even though he'd put me up to it, he'd kill me anyway: schizophrenia.

Or maybe he never meant for me to have sex with her, maybe he just wanted me to keep her company while he went bowling, play a board game with her or something, not fuck her. In which case he'd still kill me: miscommunication.

Whatever happened, there was a good chance I would die. So I made a rule: I wouldn't try to rape or kill Bryce's wife, and at the slightest hint of danger I would run away. This was a good rule, and still is, and if more people followed it the world would be a wonderful place.

I went to the door that Tuesday night with a plan. I would knock, and as soon as the door opened I would say, "Hello, my phone is broken." Whatever happened, it would be said. I was fully prepared to have those be my last words. If Bryce's bipolar pendulum had swung to homicide and he answered the door with a .12 gauge, if his keenly perceptive wife—unaware of my no-rape no-kill rule—was waiting with a can of mace and a meat cleaver, I would go down bravely, having said my piece. They would have been good last words. "Hello, my phone is broken." That pretty much would have summed me up.

They lived in a basement apartment on the side of the building. They had their own entrance, a side door that led out to some steps and the sidewalk where the Dumpsters were. That was where they'd toss my body after all of it was done.

I knocked on the door, and just as I had decided to run away she opened it.

She didn't have a meat cleaver, or a can of mace.

She was younger than Bryce and had dark blond hair, short and curly. She looked like someone I'd seen before, someone on a commercial, one for bathroom cleansers or soap. One of those women. She was wearing a navy blue bathrobe, maybe that was why.

"Hello, my phone is broken," I said, suddenly realizing what an ass I was. This was my epitaph? Fuck.

Her face was an absolute blank. I watched her bottom lip but it didn't move, and her blue eyes, a few shades lighter than her bathrobe, didn't shift or waver. She had long eyelashes that beat in slow motion like the wings of a giant bird as I waited for her to pull a tommy gun from under her robe. Her face was a white sheet of paper with no words or punctuation. My paper face said, "Hello, my phone is broken" in very small type, and there was a fucking huge question mark in tiny parentheses taking up the rest of the page. The incongruity between the question mark and the parentheses was so great that it was comical, or it was very afraid.

Without changing her expression she turned, crossed the room, and went through another door.

After standing in the doorway for a while, I went in. My mind worked feverishly. She was in a bathrobe, but her hair was dry. Maybe I was just there to fix the shower. But I didn't have any tools. Why didn't I bring tools?

There was still a good chance I would die. I crossed the room trying to think of more last words, better ones, but I couldn't think of any. They had shabby furniture but a nice TV. A big one. I wanted to see what was on, see if they had HBO. I went through the other door.

It was the bedroom. She was on the bed and her robe was on the floor. A ceiling fan was spinning overhead. The lights were already off and I shut the door behind me.

And then there was some sex. Technically, at least. Mechanically speaking, it was sex. Really we were just naked and smacking into each other. We were like two dead fish being slapped together by an off duty clown, swinging us by our tails, both of us slippery and cold, our eyes open and glassy, looking away.

That's about how passionate it was. Not that I'm much interested in passion. I always think of sex as somehow being orchestrated by an off duty clown, one who's taken off the wig but not the makeup, and he's in a T-shirt and sweat pants but he's still got on the big fucking shoes for some reason. Whenever I have sex or remember it afterwards, even when I fantasize about it, he is there. But this was disinterested even by my standards. The only thing saving us from travesty was that we were too sloppy and uncoordinated to be formulaic.

And then it was done. We were both on our backs, and still the only words between us were "Hello, my phone is broken." I wanted to ask her what was going on, why her husband had paid me $200 to have off duty clown sex with her, and if either of them planned on killing me for it. But she hadn't said a word yet, and I wasn't about to start talking.

This was a game, one I'd played hundreds of times before. Or eleven times actually, not counting her. It was like chess, but much more complicated because both of us were nude. Eventually she had to say something, had to spill everything, and then I would win. All I had to do was wait.

Then she broke.

"You should go," she said.

A brilliant tactical maneuver.

I tried to mask my utter confusion and feign some dignity as I got dressed, but it didn't work. It was dark though, and I don't think she was even looking at me. I was doing it more for myself anyway.

I tried to keep my voice low and coarse when I said goodbye, like I was a lifelong smoker. And I did. I counted this as a victory. She didn't say anything, so I just left. It was that night, out alone in a hotel bar, that I stole the first saltshaker. And then I stole three more.

It hadn't happened in years. Not that I could remember anyway. And yet there I was, sitting before some asshole detective under that bright police spotlight, my face blowing up red because of an offhand comment that could have meant anything. And that was the problem.

"Are you blushing?" Sikes asked, smiling caustically. "You have a crush on me or something sweetheart?"

"Yes," I said, and looked at him warmly.

He didn't blink, and his smile only changed slightly. If he hated fags, or if he found me at all becoming, he did a good job of hiding it.

"I think I know why you were blushing," he said.

"I'm not blushing, it's just hot in here."

"I think it's a little chilly actually."

"You're not sitting under a spotlight."

"You think that's a spotlight? I'll show you a spotlight!"

I did not know what to say.

He leaned back in his chair like he'd just bested me in a contest I did not know we were having.

"Now what did I say that made you get all flushed and rosy pink?" he said. "Do you remember?"

"I still think it's the spotlight."

"I think I mentioned something about married women. What do you have to say about that?"

"Not too much," I said, holding my voice steady.

"Oh come on, you can tell me."

"I don't think I can."

"Well let me do it for you," he said seriously, leaning forward in his chair. "I think you have a deaf girl fetish. And I think you had a perverted little crush on a married one who turned up dead. That's what I think."

He leaned back in his chair and looked at me. I felt immediately at ease. If there was anything to know, he didn't know it either.

Doug was crying again. The bus door had smashed him up pretty good this time. He showed me the dents in his head. When he asked if I wanted to touch them, I said no. Even worse, as he lay on the ground—dizzy, sobbing, a shell of a man—and as the crowd gathered around him, someone said, "Hey! He got his head stuck in the door two weeks ago. It's the same guy! It's Bus Door Head!" and some people laughed.

Bus Door Head. It was mean, juvenile and stupid. It hardly even made sense. I was rolling. Luckily I was laid back in the chair with a latex dental dam jammed halfway down my throat so the laughing made it sound like I was choking instead. Doug shoved a suction hose underneath the latex and I was nearly asphyxiated.

"I just don't understand why. Why does this keep happening to me?" he said. And Doug cried like the girl in the *After School Special* who hates high school and boys and life. He didn't understand, but I did. It was obvious to me. This was how Doug's life was, how it had always been I imagined, and how I knew it would always be. He just had that look. Game show hosts, mountain people, those Masai tribesmen who are on every other fucking cover of *National Geographic*, women who say, "Why would I ever get married, I've got cats!" and amputees. You know just by looking at them who they are. You could pick them out of a lineup. And if you had to pick Bus Door Head out of a lineup, you would always pick Doug.

He had strawberry blond hair. That's enough right there. That's all you need to know. If you're a man with strawberry blond hair and you're not in the circus or a Viking, odds are you have not found your place in life and never will. Doug's strawberry blond hair hung down in limp curls that always looked like they were wet, like he was an out of work Hasidic Jew who just didn't give a shit anymore. But then he also had the monk's tonsure up top where male pattern baldness had started its slow, inexorably humiliating crawl. Doug's head was an aesthetic and theological mess. And he had a mustache. It was too big and too ragged and trying too hard to compensate for what he'd already lost up top, and it was a few shades more strawberry than blond. He looked like the star of a new "Would you leave your child alone with this man?" pedophile awareness campaign, one that would be very effective.

Damn good dentist though. Damn good. And he let me pay my bills in installments, which hadn't started yet.

"I know you're good for it," he said.

If it weren't for his fainting spells I'm sure he would've had more patients. I never saw anybody else in there but me. Not everyone had my kind of time. The constant fits and iced tea breaks made every appointment a daylong affair. Except for the crying it was very European.

"I mean, Bus Door Head?" he said, tears draining into his mustache. "I'm sorry!" and he ran out of the room with his face in his hands, leaving me to take the fucking dental dam out of my mouth. Marlene came in and we were both laughing at Doug. After some sign language pantomime of the bus door squashing his head, we talked about her husband. His name was Brian and he was deaf too. I assumed that meant they had a lot in common and that they'd always have plenty to talk about.

So, we're deaf huh?

Yeah, how about that.

Yeah.

They'd met at a deaf disco, which I thought was an oxymoron but it wasn't. She told me it was a club where they pump the music up ear-bleeding loud and have sets of strobe lights and fog that smells like raspberries. Everyone turns up their hearing aids and dances to the whispers of music or the waves of bass, or they dance to the lights, or to the music they can't hear because even with their hearing aids they're still fucking deaf, so they dance to nothing whatsoever. I imagined it looked like the piano breakdown of a Charlie Brown special. And then when the raspberry fog rolls, everyone grinds on each other and starts making out. A really fucked up Charlie Brown special.

She'd met him there, in the raspberry fog, and they'd been married for almost two years. It wasn't going so good. Both of you being deaf isn't even enough anymore. That's what the world has become. He was nice but lazy, and often jealous. With good reason, because she was cheating on him. She'd met the other guy a few weeks ago at a karaoke bar.

What were you doing at a karaoke bar?

I was singing, stupid.
Singing? You're fucking deaf, remember?

So what! I can still sing! she signed. And then she shouted "YOU KNOW I WISH THAT I HAD JESSIE'S GIRL!—DUH NUH NUH NUH NUH NUH NUH NUH—JESSIE'S GIRL!—DUH NUH NUH NUH NUH NUH NUH NUH—WHERE CAN I FIND A WOMAN LIKE THAT!"

"Jessie's Girl," by Rick Springfield. The "duh nuh nuh nuh" was the guitar part. She even sang the guitar part. The whole thing was loud and atonal and slurred together and off the beat, and she was clapping and dancing around as she sang. She was so happy. It was and remains the most tragic thing I have ever heard. The guy who watched the Hindenburg go down had nothing, nothing on Marlene's version of "Jessie's Girl."

I have always thought of people as punch lines. I laugh at everyone, all the time. I laugh when they fall down, no matter how old they are, even if they break their hip and they're my grandmother. Jesus my mom was fucking pissed. I laugh when they just miss their bus and then run after it waving their arms in a futile attempt to make the driver stop, and when he doesn't it means they'll be late for something very important. I especially laugh when they have nervous breakdowns. Sometimes I think about that footage of Jim Bakker being led away in handcuffs as he whimpers and goes fucking insane and I have to lie down to keep from fainting. The Other Sister and I Am Sam are two of the funniest movies ever made. I can't even walk into a McDonald's, not even to steal a saltshaker. All those people stuffing double cheeseburgers into their greedy mouths are just big fat sloppy sight gags to me. I was kicked out of my reading circle in third grade for laughing at a girl who couldn't sound out her sentences. Years later she told me that I was singularly responsible for the stutter she'd later developed, and for her intense shyness and low self-esteem. The important thing was that I'd made a difference in her life. I have always found the misfortunes of others hilarious, because they're not me. If there's such a thing as karma I'm fucking doomed.

But really it's condescending and patronizing not to make fun of someone because they're old or stupid or crippled or morbidly obese. Banged up people don't want your pity. They just want to be treated like everyone else. Mockery, when done without prejudice or discretion, can be a form of respect. It's the closest we'll ever come to true equality.

But even I had to draw the line somewhere. Some line at least. And laughing at Marlene's deaf rendition of "Jessie's Girl" was it. A great shadow of conscience fell upon me. And it was cold, and felt like shame. I couldn't speak. Thank christ for sign language.

You sing this at karaoke?

Sometimes. Why?

I prayed that the crowd, if not as kind as me, was at least discreet.

How did you meet your boyfriend?

I sang "Hey Mickey" and when I was done he bought me a drink.

Jesus.

Is he deaf too?

No. He can hear everything.

Jesus.

He must be a real jackass.

Shut up! He's nice, and much better looking than my husband.

Who would win in a fight, this guy or your husband?

My husband, easy. He's crazy. He used to be in the army.

They let deaf guys in the army? Fucking A.

Does your husband know about your boyfriend?

No way! He'd kill me if he did. But he always asks me, "Where are you going? Who are you going out with? Where were you all night?" I think he follows me sometimes. It's so annoying.

That makes you mad?

Yeah.

You're mad because he's jealous?

Yeah, it's so annoying.

Maybe he's jealous because you're cheating on him, dumb ass.

No, he'd be jealous even if I wasn't, so why not cheat on him? she signed.

There are chickens, there are eggs, there are deaf girls singing karaoke. Nothing makes sense anymore.

Then it was my first day of work. At Gwen's company, Panopticon Insurance. I was a temp. A woman from human resources took me around to all the cubicles for introductions.

"This is Shane! He's your new temp! He comes highly recommended!"

"So nice to meet you!"

"Great to have you on the team!"

"Welcome aboard!"

"They're really throwing you right in, huh? Headfirst, har har!"

Yeah, har har. I tried to fake a smile but all I could do was wince and grit my teeth and groan a hello that sounded like Ed McMahon after a massive stroke. It was horrifying. Khaki pants and polo shirts and exclamation points at the end of every sentence. Each introduction was like a kick in the groin. When someone made a bad joke it was like they'd taken a running start. I had to drop to one knee after this pale turtle-looking man with a huge Adam's apple and a headset touched his finger to his earpiece and said, "Houston, we have a new temp."

I would never be able to have children.

My job was to sort, collate and alphabetize all the insurance forms that came in every day, and then send them to the records department for filing. But sorting, collating and alphabetizing are three different words for the same thing really, so by doing nothing I was already two-thirds of the way done. I was efficient.

On my first day I tried to alphabetize for about ten minutes, but being twenty-eight years old and not severely retarded I really couldn't justify it to myself so I stopped. Then I pretended to alphabetize, but that was too hard. It's the same as actually working except you get nothing done, which is more satisfying philosophically but still its own kind of work. The fucking fascists didn't give me Internet access, so mostly I just threw the insurance forms in the garbage and slept in the bathroom. Always in the handicapped stall.

It was clean, spacious, and down at the end of the row against the wall so you couldn't have guys shitting against you on two fronts. Like my grandmother said, "In the bedroom and the bathroom, never get outflanked." I was six years old. God she was a pig. But it was good as far as stalls go, with those bars on the walls that make you feel like you're a quadriplegic learning to walk again, or a ballerina. And it was always empty because most regular people feel too bad to use it, like they'd be screwing some crippled guy who'd have to shit his pants because he's too handicapped to sit in a regular stall. But all the handicapped people are at home, being handicapped. They're not working at insurance companies. When was the last time you saw a guy in a wheelchair using the copy machine? Use your fucking head.

So there I was every day, pants down, legs splayed out, arms limp at my sides, head back against the wall, my mouth hanging open, unconscious. I wanted to get a picture of myself like that, put it on a poster saying "Hey Corporate America, Fuck You!" It would be to disillusioned office douche bags what that John Belushi *Animal House* poster was for dipshit college students. I would finally be famous for sleeping on a toilet bowl with my pants pulled down, just like I'd always dreamed.

The only thing you can do as a temp is hide somewhere until it's time to go home, and the bathroom is the best place. If anybody ever asked me where I'd been all day I could answer truthfully, and if they had the audacity to ask why I'd spent my entire day in the handicapped stall I'd say, "Explosive diarrhea. I saw blood." Five words and that motherfucker would never even look at me again.

But nobody ever asked, because nobody really cares. As long as you're not sitting at your desk assembling an assault rifle or jerking off to the Internet—pants down, literally masturbating—people assume you're somewhere doing something for somebody. Nobody knows what anyone else does all day in an office. Most people don't know what they do themselves.

It was a good place to hide, but I did not like sleeping in a bathroom all day. It was a fucking men's room for christ's sake. Bad things happen in those bowls. The stench and the groans and the splashing sounds made me sad. And that kind of thing stays with you, all day. My lunches were always ruined. Lunch, as a meal for me, has never really been the same. And I began to develop a kind of bathroom narcolepsy so that whenever I sat on a toilet I'd start nodding off, even if I wasn't tired. I was Pavlov's mongoloid third cousin from that other experiment. His name was Iggy. He died forgotten and alone. And that kind of thing is fine if you're at home or in a fancy restaurant, but if you pass out in a bus station bathroom you wake up engaged to some dude in a straw hat named Maynard, and that's no good. Whatever happened, I wasn't blowing anybody.

Despite what the manufacturers say, you don't really get a solid sleep sitting on a toilet. My neck was always crooked and the flush handle bruised my spine, and I could only sleep for half an hour at a time before the tingling in my strangled legs got so bad that it knifed me awake. I had frequent nightmares, usually about vampires or dinosaurs who were chasing me, and I couldn't run away because of my bad legs. Sometimes I'd wake up shouting. God knows what anyone outside the stall thought was going on. My nerves were shot. And whenever I'd go to stand up my still-asleep legs would give out from under me and I'd have to use the ballerina bars or else I'd fall down.

Then it was like the Special Olympics trying to get back to my cubicle, Terry Foxing it down the hallway and falling into my chair, where I'd rub the backs of my legs and try to get the blood flowing again. And when it did I'd go back in and take another nap. I was afraid I might be developing varicose veins or juvenile diabetes. Something. Cutting off circulation to both legs for eight hours every day can't be good for anybody. Still, it was less humiliating than sitting at a desk and alphabetizing insurance forms. Somehow, it was.

*   *   *

I was standing in the hallway, halfway between my cubicle and my handicapped stall, not sure which was which really, leaning up against the wall like a drunk in the daytime hoping no one would notice me because I could fall down at any moment.

It was early on, before I knew the physiology of sleeping on a toilet bowl and its effects, and what I needed to do to counteract them: how long to hold on to the quadriplegic bars before trying to walk on my own, how to mazimize my momentum without tripping over my dead legs, how to use my lack of balance to my advantage, which I never really figured out. It was all a matter of timing and rhythm, like tap dancing. In those first few days I knew how to shuffle ball step, but I was wearing the wrong shoes.

So I leaned there, my palm flat on the wall, pretending to feel the texture of the smooth paint with my fingertips because I couldn't think of anything else I'd conceivably be doing in that pose. My head was still ragged from fitful, tormenting toilet sleep. I had dreamt of vampires who were riding dinosaurs. I was still not convinced it wasn't real. And then I saw something round the corner up ahead. A dark shape lurching towards me, flailing and stomping and swinging a machete. And it was closing fast.

It was like every nightmare I'd ever had as a child, the monster chasing me down and me paralyzed, powerless to run or yell for my mommy. And I would have yelled for my mommy then, in the hallway of that insurance company, if my throat hadn't been completely closed off and dammed shut. The sound in my head was like the Nazi at the end of *Raiders of the Lost Ark* who screams like a woman before he melts, and I'm sure I had the same look on my face.

I was petrified. As it came closer in its frantic lurch I saw that it was a man. An obviously insane man with a massive puff of black hair, like Art Garfunkel gone mad and brunette. He was wearing an army flak jacket and camouflage pants and huge black boots that slapped the carpeted floor like they were cobbled out of cinder blocks. His legs were wide apart like he was permanently bowlegged and he had to swing each one to get it moving. In his hand was a pair of long pruning shears.

Amazingly he didn't plunge them into my chest. Not even by accident. He spastic-stepped past me, flailing his arms like he was at the end of a power-walking marathon, not even slicing open my head as he went, a palsied cowboy sidling into the sunset.

"Mommy," I whispered, and collapsed in a heap on the floor.

Later I found out his name was Carl. He came in sometimes to water the plants people had in boxes on their cubicle walls, and he'd cut off the dead leaves when it came to that. Rumor had it he'd been in the war and taken some shrapnel in the hip and the head, that's why he was all banged up.

This was our first conversation:

"Hi," he said, standing behind me in my cubicle and scaring the crap out of me.

"Hey." I was staring at his machete pruning shears. "How's it going?"

There was a gut-wrenching silence for about thirty seconds. We stared at each other. Or his one eye stared at me while the other one wandered around in its socket, drifting over my head and swinging side to side like a pendulum. God, war is hell. I wanted to throw myself onto his shears and end it finally, on my own terms at least.

"My name is Carl," he said eight years later, "with two *a*'s."

"Oh, like c-a-a-r-l?" Maybe he was Norwegian.

"No, k-a-r-a-l. Like Karal. I water the plants and cut them."

"Oh, okay. Nice. . . ." We looked at each other. "I don't, have any plants."

"Okay, bye."

Karal was a terrible gardener. He'd forget to water the plants one week then hack the shit out of them the next. Nobody ever said anything to him though. They left him alone. He'd earned the right to be a terrible gardener by defending his country, and freedom. God bless Karal, and America too.

That next Tuesday when I went to Bryce's wife's door I didn't die, and I didn't die the Tuesday after that either. There was a succession of Tuesdays where I wasn't murdered. It eventually got to the point where my first thought after waking up Tuesday mornings wasn't, "Soon, I will be dead." And that was nice.

It was always mostly the same. She'd open the door in her bathrobe, stare through me long enough to make me uncomfortable no matter how much cold detachment I'd practiced in my bathroom mirror beforehand, then she'd go into the other room and leave me to follow. Sometimes her blue bathrobe looked brighter, like she'd just washed it with a new kind of detergent, and I thought this might be a sign that these would be special nights. But they weren't. I'd stopped saying my last words after that first Tuesday, and I hadn't been able to think of any others, so I said nothing at all.

"You should go," was all she ever said.

Still, after a few Tuesdays, just from sheer repetition, the sex had marginally improved. We were still dead fish being swung by an off duty clown, but we weren't just any kind of fish. And even if we weren't two majestic salmon, glistening in the sun as we leaped up a waterfall into the mouth of a huge fucking grizzly bear, we were at least tuna. Someone, somewhere would be glad to catch and eat us. And on rare Tuesdays we were canned tuna, fitting together, stackable, on sale two for one if you had a coupon. For a few moments at least. And the off duty clown yawned as he put us on a high shelf in his kitchen and fixed himself a drink.

I didn't mind so much lying around afterwards, watching the ceiling fan, waiting for her to tell me to leave. Of course I wanted to know what the fucked up situation between her and Bryce was, and why I'd become a part of it, and if I should start fearing death again, but I wasn't about to ask. I was in no hurry to find out really. This was good enough for me. I'd already stiffed Bryce $300 on the rent instead of two, figuring he wouldn't want to haggle over the price we'd agreed upon for me to fuck his wife. And he didn't. If I was still alive at the end of the month I wouldn't pay at all. Until then I'd keep coming back every Tuesday just to see what would happen. All I knew was that soon I'd be told to go home, which was reassuring.

Then one Tuesday, after some fleeting canned tuna sex, she said, "So tell me about yourself." Matter of fact, like we just happened to be sitting next to each other at a dinner party. Like we were meeting for the first time. And maybe we were.

Luckily it was dark and she couldn't see the shock on my face, or the panicked happiness that came after it. She wasn't looking at me, but I was still glad it was dark.

"When I was seven years old," I said, "I thought I was a superhero. My name, was Leaf Man."

"Clever," she said.

"I wasn't the brightest kid on the block, but I had the most faith." I let that stand alone for a few seconds. It sounded like it was supposed to. "My superpower was that I could jump from the top of a tree and float down like a leaf, even if there wasn't a breeze."

"Your superpower was floating?"

"Have you ever watched a leaf land? They don't even bend a blade of grass on impact. They're like ninjas. They're better than cats."

She said nothing.

"So I'm up in the top of this tree in my back yard, the kind that has the helicopter seeds that fall in October, and I'm just about even with the roof of my house, two stories up. Until then I'd only been Leaf Man jumping off my bed or the coffee table into a pile of pillows, but I wasn't afraid. I remember being absolutely sure that I could float. So I stepped off the branch, and I was gone. Everything came real fast and I was getting slapped by branches and tumbling like a fucking pinball and my head was spinning and then *wham* I hit the ground. I busted some ribs and broke my leg in two places. The doctor said I was lucky. My mom said I was a horse's ass. And I knew I wasn't a superhero."

She was silent for a long time.

"Did you have a costume?" she said finally.

"Just my GI Joe Underoos. I didn't wear a shirt. I had a cape though."

"Did your mom sew it?"

"No, I made it out of taped together St. Patrick's Day napkins."

She was silent again.

"Did you really jump out of a tree?"

"Yes," I lied.

She was silent again. I wanted to leave, but I couldn't until she told me to. So I waited. This was all making a statement of some kind and I knew I'd figure out later what it was and tell myself that I'd done well under the circumstances, and that I was still cool.

"You should go."

I was careful not to hesitate or betray anything more as I got dressed and left, and I don't think that I did.

I stole fourteen saltshakers that night and woke up withered and seasoned and tenderized the next morning.

Detective Sikes must have given some hand signal that I missed, because the lights had gotten noticeably brighter and the room was fucking roasting. I didn't say anything though. I was nonchalant as always. But I could feel the sweat on my neck.

"How well did you know Marlene Burton?"

"I told you. I talked to her a few times in the office during my appointments. That was it."

"What kind of relationship did you have with her?"

"We were friends, I guess."

"So you're admitting you had a relationship with her."

"Are you kidding me?"

"Did you see her last night?"

"No."

"Where were you last night?"

"I told you. At a bar."

"What bar?"

"This bar by my house. They have happy hour from seven to ten in the morning."

"I'm talking about last night, not yesterday morning."

"I know. I was just telling you."

"Why don't you stick to answering the questions I ask you."

"Okay."

"What's the name of the bar?"

"Sooj," I said.

"The bar is called Sooj?"

"No, Sooj is the owner."

"I'm going to ask you one more time," and he folded his hands on the table, clenching his fingers so the blood rushed to the tips. "What is the name of the bar?"

"I'm not sure," I said.

"You're not sure," he repeated, then opened his manila folder and wrote something down. "So you allegedly spent all night in this bar while a girl you had an intimate relationship with died, and you don't even know the name of the place?"

I had to admit, it did seem a bit suspicious.

"We weren't intimate. I just knew her."

He opened the folder again and wrote something else. Then he flipped through some papers and pretended to read them. I knew he was doing it just to rattle me, and it was kind of working.

"How long have you lived around here?"

"About four months."

"Where were you before that?"

"Moving around mostly."

"Moving around mostly," he repeated. "You have proof of residence from these other places you lived?"

"I don't know. Maybe. I ride the bus."

"You ride the bus," he repeated. It was pissing me off. "You ever have one of your other girlfriends disappear on you right before you left town?"

And there it was. "Pin it on a drifter," Brooks mouthed beneath his mustache, fogging the tinted window. The Chief was already picking out his tie for the press conference. By the time they were finished they'd have me convicted of every unsolved murder in the country since 1994. The victims' families would finally find closure. Sikes and Brooks would get promotions. The Chief would be governor. The sacrifice of one man for the salvation of so many would be justified. It would be right. I was like Jesus after all.

"She wasn't my girlfriend," I said, whining like I was in fourth grade. "Why are you asking me all these questions? You should be talking to her husband. He's probably the one who did it."

"Did what?" Sikes said innocently, enjoying himself.

"He hits her," I said, and that made me feel like a coward all over again only worse, because I was running to tell the teacher about a bully instead of taking care of it myself.

"What makes you say that?"

"She had a black eye last weekend. She called me and said she needed help. I met her on the waterfront."

"I thought you hadn't seen her since your last dentist appointment?" He looked down at his notes. "'A month ago, maybe longer,' you said."

Fuck.

Chapter 4

In a lifetime full of humiliations, great and small, getting to that insurance company every morning was by far the most wounding.

I couldn't ride with Gwen because she said it wouldn't look professional. I think she was ashamed of me being just a temp. It was better this way. I couldn't stomach talking to her sober anyway, especially not in the morning. Riding the bus was too bourgeois and expensive, and it made me homesick for Greyhound. It was too far to walk and I was too fragile to run.

So I bought a bike. I've always liked the idea of riding a bike. It has something to do with childhood, the sound of baseball cards stuck in the tire spokes ratcheting as you pedal home just before it gets too dark. That's how I like to think of it, even though I've never seen a kid do that in my entire goddamn life. It was big back in the fifties though, when kids were stupid and didn't know how much baseball cards were worth.

But it was more than just the stupidity of an older, greater generation and the mythic nostalgia for something I'd never had. Bicycles are the perfect harmony of man and machine. You work the pedals, use your muscles to create motion, pump your legs and grip the handlebars. And then there's speed. The wind whips around you so it's the only thing you hear, and once you get going you have your own momentum and you can take your hands off the handlebars and raise your arms over your head like you're the featherweight champion of the world, or swing them at your sides like you're sprinting really fast with hardly any effort, or spread them straight out like you're flying or being crucified, like you're Meg Ryan in that movie about angels right before she gets plastered by the logging truck.

And that's exactly how I felt riding my bike. I felt like Meg Ryan, seconds from a tragic death. It was fucking harrowing.

I bought the bike from a junk shop for twelve dollars. It was an old-fashioned cruiser with a high aristocratic seat and handlebars, the kind beautiful Italian girls with perfect posture ride in films set in the 1940s, pedaling past olive groves and waving, never suspecting that war will tear their family apart and that they'll bear the child of a stoic yet kind American GI who will die heroically saving her country from itself. Something about it didn't look right, but it was the cheapest one they had and I didn't feel like shopping. I knew I had made a mistake when some dirtbag kid yelled after me on the street, "Hey faggot! Nice cruiser! My little sister has one just like it!"

It was a girl's bike. So that was a shame.

Still, I could handle the taunts of dirtbag kids, even though they really fucking pissed me off. But besides being humiliating, my Italian woman's bike was also a death trap. No matter how tight I screwed them the nuts and bolts were always loose and rattling. The handlebars shook going downhill and sitting on the too-high seat it felt like I was riding a slinky down a flight of uneven stairs. Only the front brakes worked so whenever I stopped short I was almost thrown over the handlebars, and the front brakes didn't work in the rain so I had to stop by dragging my feet on the ground like fucking Fred Flintstone.

And it rained every day I worked at that goddamn insurance company. I was forced to buy a pair of rain pants and a slicker from Goodwill. The pants were black and three sizes too big and long, and I had to pull them up to my armpits to keep them from catching in the chain. The slicker was yellow because my piece of shit bike had no reflectors and I didn't want to die riding home at night. Visibility is important. The only helmet they had was designed for an eight-year-old pinhead and the strap was already worn thin, but I bought it anyway because of safety. It's the law.

I looked like a hobo sight gag with my mix-and-match rain gear and my junk shop bike, but for a while I thought I had some local color, some neighborhood folk hero charm. People in their cars would wave and give me the thumbs-up whenever they saw me, and they wouldn't scream curses out their windows or even honk as I slid through an intersection dragging my feet, unable to stop on the slick road, causing minor traffic accidents as cars swerved to avoid vehicular homicide. I was something of a celebrity.

Until the day I caught my reflection in a storefront window. Sitting high on a girl's bike, my bulky rain pants yanked up to my neck, my shiny yellow Gorton's fisherman slicker, my tiny child's helmet like a vulcanized yarmulke on top of my head. Those smiles and thumbs-up were really saying, "Look at that retarded boy riding his bike in the rain. And all by himself too! Good for him!"

And I wept as I sailed through those intersections, the pissing rain washing away my tears. I was something of a celebrity, a neighborhood folk hero. Just not the kind I would choose.

If Tolstoy were alive today and working as a temp at Panopticon Insurance, he'd say that all insurance companies are the same, then throw himself through an eighteenth-story window and plunge to his death in a hail of glass and shattered dignity.

I worked on the eighteenth floor, but the windows were too thick.

It was all cubicles and narrow walkways formed by the walls of cubicles, so it really was all cubicles. Their paneled walls were upholstered in heavy burgundy fabric that looked like it had been cut from medieval death shrouds, and the carpeting was mausoleum headstone slab gray. The fluorescent lights in the ceiling filtered a basement morgue pallor over everything, and the frenetic light panels screwed under the cubicle shelves to illuminate the desktops were like the caged bulbs in suburban backyards that bugs fly into to die. The thick windows didn't open, so there was the constant hum of stale air being recirculated through the vents. It sounded like nighttime on a transatlantic flight, one where you're getting screwed on the time change but it doesn't matter because the plane is slowly, almost imperceptibly descending right into the fucking ocean.

These people, my teammates, they had to have known. They had to have realized, in their own small, terrified way, that something about it all was horribly wrong. That's why they packed their little cubicles with old Mardi Gras beads and postcards from far-off Hard Rock Cafes, with signs saying "You Want It When?" that had little cartoon men underneath bent over laughing at your unreasonable request, with trinkets, with framed certificates saying they'd been certified in CPR, with photographs of confused babies with big heads in frames titled "Spit Happens!" and school portraits of awkward kids with braces smiling in front of sky blue backdrops and Polaroids of dogs and fucking cats, all the shit that people and pharaohs surround themselves with to make it seem not so bad.

I knew why they did it, but that didn't make it any easier to stomach. They seemed like nice enough people in their own creepy way, and I'm sure they meant well, but that just wasn't good enough. They'd probably made some bad decisions along the way, decisions they'd long since rationalized to themselves to keep from suicide. Or maybe they'd just done what they thought they had to do to pay the bills. And that's fine. People have families and mortgages and other responsibilities. But that doesn't excuse all the goddamn misplaced enthusiasm.

Nobody there hated their job nearly as much as they should have. That always bothered me. I heard them complain sometimes, but it was the ineffectual bitching of people who didn't expect anything about their situation to ever change, and who wouldn't know what to do with themselves if it did. They were all older, rounder, more compromised versions of each other, all of them middle-aged, if not in years in appearance and aspiration. It was like time-release photography of humanity in slow decline. The mushroom cloud was Hawaiian shirt day. It was depressingly easy to picture the new girl, with her bright scarves and flipping hair thinking she was only there until she found another job at a non-profit, ten years later wearing a business suit and white sneakers as she power-walked around the building on her half-hour lunch break.

That's what I thought on a bad day. And since every day you're temping at an insurance company is a bad day, that's what I thought. It's easy to lose faith when your weekdays are draped in death shrouds and your only respite is to sleep on a toilet. It is very easy to lose faith then.

And whenever I thought I was being too hard on them, I remembered Inspiration Alley. There was proof that nice, well-meaning people would politely and eventually rob the rest of us of any reason to live. Inspiration Alley was a row of cubicles stretching from the boss's double-cube office to the inner walkway around the elevators, and it was lined with quotations. They were printed on company letterhead in large type and tacked up on the burgundy walls like mirrors in a funhouse. These were my favorites:

Some men see things as they are and say why. I dream things that never were and say why not—Robert Kennedy

Do not hurry, do not rest—Goethe

Once all struggle is grasped, miracles are possible—Mao Tse-tung

I looked around, waiting for someone to do something. Then I realized that I was someone—Anonymous

Great things are not done by impulse, but a series of small things brought together—Vincent Van Gogh

The energy, the faith, the devotion which we bring to this endeavor will light our country and all who serve it, and the glow from that fire can truly light the world—John F. Kennedy

When the way comes to an end, then change—having changed, you pass through—I Ching

If at first an idea is not absurd, then there is no hope for it—Albert Einstein

And the coup d'etat:

If a man is called to be a streetsweeper, he should sweep streets even as Michelangelo painted, or Beethoven composed music, or Shakespeare wrote poetry. He should sweep streets so well that all the hosts of heaven and earth will pause to say, here lived a great streetsweeper who did his job well—Martin Luther King

That one took two pages of company letterhead, but it was worth it.

I sometimes saw people standing there, moving their lips as they read, nodding, really understanding, clenching their fists at their sides, "Yes. Yes!" Then they went forth to be the best insurance agents the world had ever seen, for the glory of God and Panopticon. And I sat in my cubicle making a miniature gallows out of paper clips, and waited for my legs to work again.

The boss's name was Andrew, but he didn't like the term *boss*. He referred to himself as the *team facilitator*. He was blond and slight and soft-voiced, with that managerial style where you speak quietly and *ask* your employees to do things, prefacing every request with, "Could you do me a favor?" or "If you have time . . ." or "Whenever you have a moment . . ." and ending with "At your earliest convenience, of course." It's the kind of shtick where if you're a parent who tries it on their kids they grow up to be crack whores and gang-related murder statistics with no respect for anything. But it works on defeated adults because they don't have the backbone to say "Fuck you Dad" and make the obviously wrong decision.

Andrew was always nice to me. So nice that every time he saw me he'd say, "Hi Shane." He once, in a span of six minutes, said "Hi Shane" eleven times. I fucking counted. He just kept walking past my cubicle "Hi Shane . . . Hi Shane . . . Hi Shane . . ." Finally, after the tenth time, I was on my way to the bathroom. He was standing talking to somebody and as I passed he turned his head—while the other guy was in mid-sentence—and mouthed *Hi Shane*, then turned back to the conversation. It was very unsettling.

When I returned from the bathroom I went back to work on my gallows. But it is hard to make a full-size noose out of paper clips, and it takes a very long time. As it's set up, the world encourages you to do things in miniature.

If sex with the landlord's wife was like an off duty clown swinging two fish together by their tails, then sex with Gwen was that same off duty clown sitting on the splintered wooden floor of his living room with a gun in his mouth, watching a German snuff film and crying.

"You know what I like about you?" she said.

We were on our backs and her sheets were drenched with

sweat and fear and gallons of my blood. I thought my collarbone was broken, or at least torn out of its socket. And that was a shame, because it had always been one of my best features: prominent but not overbearing, shapely and subtly regal. It was the clavicle of an African queen. But not after this. Not after Gwen. She'd dug her hands in up to her knuckles and yanked up on it as she slammed herself into my pelvis, using my own body against me. I was a fuck prop in her one woman show. The critics vomited in the aisles and the ushers wept unabashedly. And I sang that Foreigner song in my head:

> *I wanna know what love is . . .*
> *I want you to show me . . .*

slow, and with emotion, as she kicked the shit out of me. I thought the irony might dampen the unbearable pain, but it gave me no comfort. I fingered my collarbone and thought of happier times.

"I like how you never bring work home with you. You leave it behind when you walk out every day."

This was not entirely true. I used to fall asleep in her bathroom all the time.

"I know you're just a temp, but still," she caught herself, thinking maybe she'd offended me, as if that was even possible, "and I know you're busy now and putting in a lot of hours, so we don't get to spend as much time together, but you're really good at separating yourself from it."

"Yeah," I said.

"I need to do that more. I need to step back and remember who I am. I hate thinking about work and stressing myself out when I'm at home and I should be relaxing." She paused, then said thoughtfully, "I need to remember that Panopticon Insurance is not my entire life."

It was one of those completely untrue affirmations people feel like they have to make every once in a while, like "This was for my lord and savior Jesus Christ," whenever somebody catches a football for a four yard gain, or "We did all we could," whenever a doctor loses a patient who's old and not famous. It's just something you say.

Because Panopticon Insurance was her entire life. It was all she ever goddamn talked about. All her friends worked there, or they were former employees who'd left on good terms with management. She went in on weekends even though she didn't have to. She fell asleep thinking about it and had nightmares where she had to make decisions even though she wasn't given all the necessary information, and hilarious dreams where she fired the corporate vice president because he wore an ugly tie. She fucking woke me up in the middle of the night to tell me that one. And I'm pretty sure she called me Panopticon during sex. More than once.

It was her entire life, and that's exactly how she wanted it to be. And that's fine. She cared about Panopticon Insurance. It was important to her. And that's nothing to be ashamed of. Which is untrue, and again just something you say.

"So I like that about you," she said again, and leaned her head on my shattered collarbone as I writhed and wilted.

"I also like that about myself," I said. Of all the things in me to admire, she picked my apathy. That's disheartening.

"Oh, I meant to tell you, marketing is having a contest to come up with a new slogan for the company. The winner gets a fifty-dollar gift certificate and a write-up in the newsletter. You're so creative, why don't you enter?"

"I'm shy," I said.

"*I* would beg to differ," and she curled her head under my chin, trying to play sexy as the pain coursed through me like I was being fucking electrocuted.

"What's the old slogan?" I said through clenched, grinding teeth.

"Panopticon Insurance: Watching Out for You, Wherever You Go."

"Chilling."

"I kind of like it. But they want to bring it into the twenty-first century, maybe say something about technology or computers, but still keep that old brand nostalgia."

"The Neo-Nazis are trying to do the same thing."

"Ha ha, real funny."

"So's the Klan."

"Could you be serious for once?"

"All right, how about Panopticon Insurance: Where Dreams Go to Die."

"If you don't want to do it that's fine," she said, annoyed, and turned over. I was very happy with myself.

She lay there, facing the wall, breathing loud through her nose to let me know that she was angry. After a few minutes of cleansing, nasal-snorting silence, she turned back towards me. She had worked through her feelings, and we could talk again. Self-help pop psychology techniques are fucking fascinating.

"So how do you like working with Martha? Isn't she great?" she said.

"Yeah. She rules."

And so did Fred and Keith and Sue and all the other faceless fuckers I didn't know who sat in the cubicles nearby. They were all on my *amazing* team and they could all help me get a full-time job if I was nice enough to them, asked if they needed any extra photocopying done or a shoeshine, or a rimjob maybe? The implication was clear. But I didn't talk to anybody. I knew them only as the ugly guy, or the fat guy who's gay, or the old woman with the stringy hair. None of them had names and I didn't want them to. I didn't want to be involved, even in the shallowest sense of the word. But I didn't tell Gwen that. I never told her about sleeping in the bathroom either. She would not have understood.

"What about Karal?" I said. "How did he ever get hired in the first place?"

"Who?"

"The banged up guy who waters the plants. Karal."

"Oh Carl! He's not really an employee. He works for the maintenance company. He must be in a union or something. But Gina in HR—"

"Who?"

"Gina? In HR? Human *Resources*? You really need to start learning the lingo Shane." And she laughed.

My god, how I loathed her.

"Anyway, Gina told me that his mother calls every Friday and says, 'Did my son do a good job this week?'"

"His mom? Jesus."

"I know! But how is Gina supposed to know? He doesn't even *work* for us!" She thought that part of it was hilarious. "One day she started crying and told Gina how he used to be an Eagle Scout and he was so handsome until this hunting accident in high school where he almost blew his head off. There was mud in the barrel of his gun and—"

"Hunting accident? I thought he was in Nam?"

"I don't think so. I think he's always been with the maintenance company. But she was crying and everything. Gina didn't even know where to transfer her! Isn't that crazy?"

I agreed that it was, in fact, fucking insane. After she had sighed her way out of laughing she said, "I should introduce you to Gina. The more people you know in HR the better."

"Human Resources," I said.

After pedaling all the way home from work in the goddamn pouring rain and almost dying at three different intersections, I realized that I'd left my keys on my desk. They were behind the stapler, wrapped in a paper towel. Goddamnit.

I'd had a rough time on the toilet that morning. I woke up kicking and holding on to the handicapped bars with both hands. I was dangling from a fucking helicopter in my dream, hanging on to the landing gear as we flew out over water. We were really high up and the pilot was jerking us all over the sky, trying to shake me off. He didn't like me for some reason. I gasped and opened my eyes as an echo clanged off the walls. I had just kicked the metal stall partition, really hard. My foot hurt. And someone was standing outside the door.

Their shoes were pointing in at me. They were probably wondering if they should knock, or say, "Is everything all right in there? Do you need any help?" But they didn't. After a second's hesitation they left, without saying a word. There are no good samaritans in a men's room. Nobody wants to help some guy off the toilet. Maybe if he's family, but even then, hire a fucking nurse or something.

I got up quick, still shaking off the dream. All I had to do was be out of the stall before anyone else came in. Then if they asked me anything I'd blame it on Karal. *Yeah, that guy who waters the plants ran past me as I walked in. I think he was crying.* But when I stood up I saw my keys sprawled out on the rancid floor in a pool of water at the base of the toilet, like they were sunning themselves in filth. They'd fallen out of my pocket during the helicopter struggle. I didn't know where all the water had come from. A pipe must have been leaking. Or. Oh god.

I ran them under the lukewarm water in the sink for a few minutes, but it wasn't enough. It would never be enough. They were tainted now, polluted with dribbled piss and splattered shit and toilet water. The unclean molecules had already attached themselves and become part of their DNA. It's how atoms work. That's why everyone hates science. I wrapped them in a paper towel like a dead pigeon and set them on my desk behind the stapler and tried not to think about them for the rest of the day. And I didn't. Which is why they were still there and I was outside my locked door, half-drowned and cursing the ugliness of the world and its bathroom floors. I hoped the cleaning people wouldn't throw them out. They'd probably be too busy stealing shit to even bother.

There was no way I was riding all the way back to work in the rain just to get my filthy keys, just to ride back home and almost die all over again. It wasn't going to happen. I thought about kicking the door in or jimmying the lock with a credit card, but I knew I didn't have it in me. To do that kind of thing you really have to believe. I settled for trying the door knob again, twice. It didn't work.

So I sat down with my back to the door and went over my options. I could go to Bryce. Whatever else was happening, he was still my landlord. It's what you do when you're locked out of your apartment. Or I could call a locksmith myself, spend the money to skip the awkward "No no, I'm not here to have sex with your wife Bryce, I just need my key" conversation. Or I could go to a bar and get drunk, then curl up on the floor in front of my door and pass out. I was already in my work clothes for the next morning. I usually wore the same thing every day anyway. It would be all right on the floor. My ass was asleep and I'd only been sitting there a few minutes. And everywhere is comfortable when you're unconscious.

I was kind of looking forward to it actually, until I walked out the front door and saw Mobo standing there under the awning, stroking his goatee. Ivan wasn't with him. For his sake I hoped he was dead.

"Bambilo!" Mobo said, smiling at me, "How you been my man?"

"Uh, pretty good. How, are you?"

"Surviving pacho, surviving. The rain has the answers, but it's making me hungry, you know?"

"Yeah, I've got to get out of here," I said, buttoning my yellow raincoat. "I'm locked out, so—"

"You locked out? You came to the right hocho. I got your key upstairs."

"Huh?"

"Bryce gave it to me."

"What? He gave you my key?"

"Come up in a few mapos camacho. I need some time to hide the bodies," he said, and laughed as he went inside.

I stood there, staring out at the rain. I felt like something had just exploded in my face, like I was the bumbling bad guy in a Disney movie, black soot dusting my cheeks and forehead, my hair blown straight up and still sizzling at the tips. But there was nothing funny about this, and it could never be seen by children. Mobo had a key to my apartment. That meant Mobo had definitely had non-consensual sex with Ivan on my salty bed, and probably in my kitchen too. I'd have to live with that knowledge from now on. And I really didn't know how to do it. Even for a man who doesn't care about anything, that's a little too much to bear.

It couldn't have been true. It just wasn't possible. I would've seen the fur, found the stains, felt the presence of evil. I would've had ghosts in my apartment after something like that. Ghosts who wept through the night in between bouts of nausea and suicide attempts. No, Mobo had not fucked a guinea pig in my bed. Or on my cutting board. He was probably just sniffing my boxers or pissing in my tub. Maybe he used my place to take shits.

No. That's not how it was. Bryce had given my spare key to Mobo because Bryce's wife kept stealing it. She liked to sneak into my apartment while I was at work and lie on my bed. Sometimes she wore one of my old T-shirts. Sometimes she went through my stuff, looking for a photo album. She wanted to sigh over what a cute kid I'd been, a cute baby. She wanted to see pictures. But I didn't have any. Then Bryce found out and he put a stop to it the only way he could: Mobo. She couldn't get past Mobo. Dudes who fuck guinea pigs are the modern equivalent of that three-headed dog and Medusa and all those other Greek monsters. That's how far we've come in a few thousand years.

So that's what happened. That's why Mobo had my key. It wasn't true of course, but I didn't care. I believed what I had to. I'd lived with bigger lies before, but none more important.

I went upstairs and knocked on Mobo's door.

"Surprise surprise," he said, shaking his head. He was wearing a kilt, and he didn't have a shirt on. His white albino chest was blinding, like the light you see when you die just before you go to hell for all eternity. "Is this business or pleasure?"

"Uh, remember I just talked to you downstairs? About my key?"

"Ah, what we talk about and what we mean are always two different things compodro."

"No they're not," I said, but he had already turned back inside. He left me standing at the open door, like Bryce's wife always did. Déjà vu makes me fucking sick sometimes.

I took a deep breath and held it. Then I stepped inside.

His apartment was much less like a dungeon than I expected. Except for little, leathered Ivan shivering in the corner, shackled to the wall in thick medieval chains, it wasn't like a dungeon at all. There was a leopard-print throw rug, and four upholstered seats against the wall that looked like they'd been stripped from an old theater. There was a feathered dream catcher hanging from the ceiling like a useless chandelier. There were birds chirping and other muted animal calls, and water was falling around me under a light hush of music. It sounded like a lady was playing the harp in a rain forest. It was very peaceful. Until an elephant blasted its fucking trumpet call so loud I thought it was smashing through the wall.

"You want some avocado?" Mobo said, standing in the center of the room under the dream catcher.

But I couldn't respond. I was transfixed by the mural that desecrated his far wall. Mobo and Ivan—a full-sized, *Planet of the Guinea Pigs* Ivan—were side by side at the end of a craps table in a casino. Ivan was bent over the table, leaning in. He'd just thrown the dice. Furry cleavage spilled out of his cocktail dress. It was red, like his lipstick. Mobo was beside him, naked from the waist up and wearing a loincloth. He was tan and ripped and glistening, flexing his painted-on biceps as he roared for a good roll. There was a wad of bills in each clenched fist and an unmistakable bulge in his loincloth. It was shaped like a fire hydrant. It cast its own shadow on the table.

"You like that?" Mobo said as I swayed and almost fainted. "One of my barrachas gave it to me. She's a kindergarten teacher."

"That's appalling."

"She's doing another one for me. Ivan's going to be the Virgin of Guadalupe, isn't that right? If you ever sit still for your head shots, bitch!" he yelled at little, cowering Ivan as I pretended to be deaf and invisible.

"So, you want a sprinkle on your avocado? A little tinkata?" Mobo said.

"What? No. I don't want any avocado."

"You want the tour? I don't have a shower curtain but my futon is brand new," he said, and motioned towards a curtain of beads hanging in an open doorway, where he kept all the torture machines and lube.

"Christ, no. I just want my key."

"Ha ha, don't be shy mondurro. Have a seat, as the Indians did." He pointed to his leopard-print rug, then disappeared through the curtain of beads into his unholy bedroom. There was no way I was sitting on his fucking floor. I was pretty sure the rug had syphilis. I collapsed in one of the theater chair aisle seats instead and put my hands on my knees like a girl wearing a skirt in public for the first time.

Ivan was staring at me. Strapped in his slave hood, he twitched his nose continuously, furiously. It seemed deliberate, like he was spelling out something in Morse code. *Kill me* maybe, over and over again, like that deformed soldier in the *Metallica* video. If it was sign language I may have felt compelled to act, but I didn't know Morse code, so I had an excuse. I'm sorry Ivan.

When Mobo came out he was wearing a ripped T-shirt, and carrying a briefcase in each hand.

"You like the white man's chairs eh?" he said, nodding. "All right, let's get down to business chapo."

He sat down in the seat right next to me, and as he did his bare knee slid out from under his receding kilt and touched the back of my hand just as a monkey screamed out of the rain forest like he was swinging in the fucking window. Too many unsettling things were happening at once. I would need a sanitarium, or some time in the country at least.

"So what you need?" he said, balancing a briefcase on each knee.

"I need my key."

"Of course, of course. I can help. I know what you seek. Clarity."

He stood up and unhooked the dream catcher from the ceiling.

"Just relax," he said, dangling it over my head. And then, as I sat paralyzed in disbelief, he chanted "Humma humma humma humma" while he shook the dream catcher down past my lap to my feet, then worked his way back up to my head. After the third pass over my balls I had to speak.

"Just open that one," I said.

"Which one?"

"That one," and I pointed to the briefcase closest to me.

"You see? What did I tell you?" he said as he re-hung the dream catcher and sat down. "You just have to listen to your machoso. Always."

He popped the briefcase open and inside was an M-80, two sparklers and a pack of those shitty black pellets that turn into ash snakes when you light them.

"My babies." He was delighted. "Los niñatas. You won't find a better stash outside of *Tijuana*," he said, accenting it like he'd been kicked in the throat between syllables.

"I just want my key."

"Don't worry. The first taste is always free."

"I don't want a taste," I said.

"We all want a taste."

"They're fireworks, you can't eat them."

"A taste."

"Fine. Give me the M-80."

"Ha ha, I like the way you think dando. Have another taste. One more. You want it, I can tell. You're hungry now."

"Give me a sparkler."

"I knew it, I knew it," he said.

What he didn't know was that I was planning to catheterize him with it if he didn't give me my goddamn key. He had about three minutes. I was that close to madness. Being in the jungle really does drive you insane. The effects are almost immediate. A pterodactyl shrieked out of the rain forest in agreement.

"Something else I want to show you," he said, digging in his kilt with both hands.

I clenched the sparkler in my fist, but he was unsnapping a button and reaching into a pocket. Kilts have pockets now apparently. Weirdos are finally getting practical.

He pulled out my key. It was dangling from the end of a candy bracelet. I almost wept.

"I trust you with this," he said, holding it up for me to see.

"It's my key."

"Even better choco," and he dropped it into my open hand. It hit my palm like another man's used condom.

"I'm getting out of here," I said, already out of my chair and walking towards the door.

Ivan squealed in his chains as I passed, but it wasn't like the frenzied shrieks of penetration that I heard through my ceiling all those nights as I tried to smother myself with my pillow. This was a whimper, quiet and pleading. This was a cry for help. I couldn't even look at him.

"I'll see you again chachi! You know it!" Mobo yelled after me as I rushed out the door.

Back in my apartment, I wanted to wrap myself in paper towels. I didn't know what Mobo had touched, where Ivan had been positioned. I figured I should at least delouse my stuff, spray some Lysol maybe. But I sat on my bed instead. Then I laid down. My clothes were still wet but I didn't bother changing them. It was no use. There's only so much you can do in a world as thoroughly defiled as this, and even that's not worth the trouble.

And then, to redeem the filth and shame of life, just like Cinderella I was invited to the ball. A deaf birthday party at Marlene's house. She was turning thirty-four. I didn't bring a present.

It wasn't Tuesday and I had nowhere else to be, but I didn't plan on staying. Even if I was having a good time I'd have to leave before they sang "Happy Birthday." For humanity's sake. If there was karaoke I'd have to kill myself immediately.

I had no idea what to expect. I didn't know people even had birthday parties anymore. Not in their houses. And everybody at this one would be deaf. I would dominate musical chairs. Marco Polo would be a travesty. There would be no blindfolds for the piñata or pin the tail on the donkey because that has to fuck up your equilibrium if you already can't hear. People would be falling all over each other. I hadn't been to a birthday party in a long, long time.

Marlene either lived in #6 or #16. Number six was a small white house that looked like it was built out of cardboard and held together by paint, but really it was built out of wood and held together by nails just like every other goddamn house in the world. I stood outside at the bottom of the steps, not sure what to do. It didn't look like there was a party inside. But then, it never does, does it.

As I was considering this, someone busted through the front door like the motherfucking Kool-Aid Man and barreled down the steps. He had tightly curled hair set way back on his scalp and his forehead was the size of a drive-in movie screen. He looked deaf and pissed off. I stepped aside as he bulled past me, his big head tucked into his shoulders. He stared me broad in the face as he passed, but said nothing. He had on a green sweatshirt with the sleeves pushed up to his elbows and a pair of green sweat pants that were three shades lighter than his shirt. I definitely had the right house.

I stepped through the open front door, lightly, like I was stepping onto a trampoline.

Marlene was standing just inside with her back to me, agitated and flailing her hands at a guy and some lady. Her neck was bright red and she moved her hands like I did when I was speaking angry sign language gibberish, but she was obviously making some kind of sense because the two people were listening and nodding, and the guy signed *No fucking way!* after Marlene threw up her hands. I was very impressed with myself for picking it up.

He tapped one of Marlene's furious hands and motioned towards me. She turned around scowling, her hair swinging over her eyes, but her face shattered into a crooked smile when she saw that it was me.

"SHANE!" she shouted.

"Aaaaaye!" I said, and made hand gestures like I was Italian.

Why are you mad? I signed, just so everyone would know that I could. The guy and the lady smiled. Nice.

My husband's an asshole.

Was that him? And I thumbed out the door.

Yeah, fucking asshole.

He looked like a giant string bean, I signed, and the three of them burst out laughing loud and off-key. Ahh, the laughter of the deaf. I was a hit at my first deaf party. I was popular among the hearing impaired.

This is Shane, Marlene signed, laughing.

They both signed *Hello*.

Hello fuckheads, I signed back.

They were dumbfounded. The lady looked offended and I think the guy wanted to punch me in the face. Shit. Too much too soon. I had squandered all my hearing-impaired credibility. My reputation would never recover.

Marlene turned to them and signed something so quick that I didn't catch it. They all laughed, then smiled at me like I was retarded, which Marlene may have told them I was. I didn't care. At least I didn't have to fight anyone. I had a theory that while the blind are given super hearing to compensate for their condition, the deaf are given super strength, like Lou Ferrigno, and I was in no hurry to find out if I was right.

Weirdo, Marlene signed as she shook her head and grabbed my arm, leading me into the house.

What did you say to them about me?

I told you you were retarded.

I knew it.

Go out to the backyard, weirdo. There's beer. I'll be out soon, and she pointed me through the kitchen towards the back door.

Everyone I passed was talking unbelievably fast with their hands and mouthing things to each other so quickly I could only pick out stray words and phrases. A man said *yes*. A woman said *please*. Another man said *I don't know* and laughed. It was like watching Telemundo after four years of high school Spanish. I didn't know what was going on. And there I was believing I could translate for the United Nations. It was very humbling. The Lebanese ambassador could still go fuck himself.

I couldn't believe there were so many of them. I figured it would just be Marlee Matlin and a man-child in overalls or two, but there were like forty people standing around, all of them deaf. It was unprecedented. There was a low hum of mumbling and motion as people's mouths and hands moved in tandem, and it made me think of hummingbirds and Japanese gardens though I did not know why. It was kind of beautiful.

But I was panicking. I felt like the new kid at a middle school dance where everyone knew everyone except me. I was different. I didn't fit in. And it was true, which was very refreshing. As an adult there are so few situations where you can legitimately feel like you're at a middle school dance and not hate yourself for being melodramatic. It was fascinating to see how little I'd grown.

Then I saw Doug standing over by the keg, smiling at everyone, blissfully ignorant of how awkward the scene really was. Yeah they had a keg. Deaf people fucking party.

"Shane!" Doug called out as he saw me, cracking the silence like a gunshot that only I could hear. Despite myself I was overjoyed to see him. He was the fat kid in math club who played the tuba and licked the nosepads of his glasses, but I didn't care. Whoever said any port in a storm was standing alone at a middle school dance.

"This is a great party huh? I feel like I'm back at dental college!"

Standing alone by the keg. Again. Ahh Doug.

"You been here long?" I whispered, not wanting to show off.

"About an hour and a half." He was speaking at a regular volume but it sounded incredibly loud.

"Where are the cups?"

"I don't know if there are any left. Here, you can take this one." Doug had an extra cup stacked over the one he was drinking from. "Just in case I felt like fisting, ha ha ha."

I offered up a silent prayer, pleading that he'd really meant to say "double fisting." Then I tried to ignore the image of Doug's beer-soaked child molester's mustache brushing over the lip of my cup, bristle by strawberry blond bristle. But I could not. The beer tasted like kiddie porn, and I had to drink it. I felt dirty and sad. For the children, and for myself.

Doug had mastered the art of talking to people who weren't interested in what he had to say, so it didn't seem to bother him that I was obviously not paying attention.

"He's confusing a bicuspid with a canine and he's going to lecture *me* on how to fill a cavity? I don't care if he was a dentist in the Korean War, we've had a few changes since then. I mean, technology? Hello? Ha ha ha. I don't mean to talk about my other patients like that. Must be the brew."

The brew was Coors Light, and I was drinking a full cup for every sip that Doug took. And I was deliberately drinking slower than I wanted to, so I wouldn't fall down. I held his cup for him while he bent down to tie his shoe and the plastic was damp and warm as piss. He'd been on the same beer all night, and he had sweaty palms. Gross.

"I'm thinking about putting a speaker in the office so I can listen to some tunes while I work. Nothing too heavy, just something I could bop to. Wayne Newton's early stuff, some

Lawrence Welk big band, maybe jazz it up with some Tiny Tim every once in a while. I like all different kinds of music. . . ."

I didn't even have to pretend I was listening with the usual "uh huh . . . ok . . . oh really? . . . uh huh . . ." prompts. He just kept going. It was like being in his office chair, only without the dental dam jammed halfway down my throat. Doug just needed someone to be there for him. Literally. He would've made a fantastic necrophiliac. And at that moment I didn't care. I just wanted someone to stand next to. With him babbling beside me I could relax and observe the scene instead of feeling awkward and alone.

Except for the sign language and the occasional outrageously loud and off-key laugh, it was just like any other party. People were standing around talking, drinking, just hanging out in somebody's backyard. There was no raspberry fog, no karaoke, no heart-rending eighties theme. It was just a regular party. I was secretly, bitterly disappointed.

But whether it was the soothing peace of all those people talking silently with their hands or the cups of Coors Light I was pounding or the hypnotic drone of Doug's inane bullshit, I felt good and happy. Above all I was utterly, utterly proud of myself for knowing sign language, even if I couldn't really understand it. I was a scholar and a gentleman, and a great human being.

". . . and I know most people would probably argue with me, but I really think Paul McCartney did his best work with *Wings*," Doug said as Marlene stumbled over and grabbed my arm.

"SHANE! COME ON!" And she pulled me away from him.

I looked back over my shoulder and Doug was smiling benevolently, as only a man who has accepted that he will always be left can.

You're drunk! I signed.

So are you!

No. I . . . am . . . GENIUS!!!

Marlene's atonal laugh rocked the backyard. I followed her into the house.

Why was your husband pissed before? I signed.

We were fighting. He said there were too many people and it was too loud. Fuck him. Come on, I want to show you something.

We went inside and when she pulled me up a flight of stairs I started thinking that maybe she wanted me to have sex with her. I was considering it. I was drunk and she was deaf. It would at least make for a good story. But I wasn't sure who I would tell. Maybe Karal, or *Penthouse.*

When she led me into her bedroom I got a little nervous because it was packed with people. I just wasn't sure I could handle a deaf gangbang, all the howls and moaning like a bag of kittens drowning in a river. But the crowd gave way to her frantically motioning hands and then we were standing before the drawing I'd done of her sitting on that heap of trash with her horse teeth and big ears. She'd framed it and hung it in her bedroom. I was so proud of myself I wanted to cry.

"GOOD WORK!" Marlene shouted as she slapped me on the back, and everyone in the room started laughing and clapping.

They were applauding me. I was famous. And I knew then what I would do for the rest of my life: caricatures of the deaf, for acclaim and standing ovations. I would win grants and go to charity events. I would be feted. Maybe I would date Marlee Matlin. I would create the United Deaf Negro College Fund in memory of a hearing-impaired black man that I had never met. PBS would do a feature on me and I would help them with their telethons. I would also try to help Jerry Lewis, but he would refuse. He was very quirky.

I raised my arms above my head and pumped my fists, giddy and triumphant and drunk. Marlene pointed at the picture, then pointed at me and the room erupted. It was fucking cacophony, claps and wailing deaf people and laughter. I was almost embarrassed by all the attention, and by all the fucked up noises they were making, but what could I do? These were my people now.

They ushered me out of the room and the crowd pushed me into the backyard where the rest of the party was, and as we spilled through the door they all looked at us, wondering why we were in hysterics. And because I know things about show business I spun around and pointed at Marlene, then swung my arm over my head and brought it down to pinch my nose so theatrically I could have been a very skinny professional wrestler. *YOU . . . STINK!!!*

Deaf people were falling all over each other. I was the funniest man in the world. Marlene was bent over laughing, her face so red I thought it would pop like a grape. The atonal swell was an uproar. Garbage bags of kittens were screeching in the cold, cold water.

I went to the *YOU . . . STINK!* well again, which I never would have done if I'd been sober. It was amateur, but I couldn't help myself. There were tears on all their faces. They were laughing themselves to death, all of them holding on to each other to keep from rolling in the grass. Marlene was struggling to stand upright and point at me, but she couldn't straighten up long enough to do it. This was exactly what I needed. This was my Academy Award.

And so what if it was all novelty. I knew that even as it was going on. It was a one-joke act and probably wouldn't last through the party without going stale, but I didn't care. For that moment I was the guy dancing in the middle of the circle that everyone wanted to watch. I was Kevin Bacon in *Footloose*, except funny and not in high school yet, and never, ever on the gymnastics team. I was popular, and that's what middle school is all about.

"Shane?" It was Doug, tapping me on the shoulder, wanting to be popular for once too.

"Yeah?"

"Everyone is laughing at you," he said.

"Yeah." I was hilarious.

Then Doug put his hand to my back and pulled off a piece of paper. I saw the Scotch tape curling off the top. There was a sign on my back. The words, in big, bold print: I'M STINK.

The already deafening laughter collapsed into full-blown hysteria. I looked over at Marlene. She'd fallen to the ground holding her stomach, saying "OW! OW!" it hurt from so much laughing. Everyone's mouth was open, gaping, coughing, hacking, sick from laughing so hard. All at me. One woman had lipstick on her teeth, bright red, which I sometimes dream about. To this day I wake up drenched and screaming.

It had to be a noise violation. Why hadn't the neighbors called anyone? Where were the fucking police? It had gone beyond laughter at that point. It was one massive blast of atonal sound, like a fucked up symphony of 3,000 car alarms going off at the same time all around me. And there was no one to press that fucking keychain button to make them stop.

*   *   *

So I'd lied to him. So what. This wasn't Sunday school. This was America. You can lie to anybody you want goddamnit. Even if they're a detective. Even if you're in some interrogation room under a goddamn spotlight. Even if a woman's dead and you're somehow the prime suspect. Fuck.

Sikes wrote something else in his manilla folder and he looked at it for a long time. The back of my neck was hot. My legs were cramping. I wanted to go back to sleep and wake up and start all over again. This time I'd get sodomized and wait for a lawyer.

Sikes closed the folder and pushed it to the middle of the table. Then he got up and left without saying anything. I wasn't sure if I was allowed to open it and read what he'd been writing or if they'd be mad at me if I did, so I just sat there and tried to think of a way out.

He came back in and sat down. I had aged years in his absence. I'd done my time already and was up for parole. I'd been a model prisoner. I was reformed. Why didn't they just let me go?

"You got anything else you'd like to tell me?" he said.

"No."

He looked at me hard.

"You got any family around here?"

"No."

"You got anybody you can call?"

"Not really," I said.

"You got anybody who gives a shit one way or the other what happens to you?"

"That's not a very nice question to ask somebody."

We looked at each other, and I thought for a second he knew that I was right.

·∴·∴· Chapter 5

I had planned to skip my Tuesday with the landlord's wife. I was still embarrassed about the bullshit Leaf Man story, even though I kept telling myself that I shouldn't be and that really I was just there for some rent-subsidized sex so who cared either way. I was not very convincing.

So I went, but only on the condition that I would trick her into telling me something about herself, something guarded and personal, which I would then use to humiliate her in a seemingly innocent and unintentional way. Then we'd be even, and we could go back to being silent and normal again.

But when I got there I didn't follow through. Because pride is stupid. And because she never gave me a chance to. I don't think I would have though, even if she did. We just had our sex and then she told me to go. Still, it felt like we had re-established something, if it felt like anything at all.

The Tuesday after that we were lying beside each other, not touching like we always did, and I was waiting for her to tell me to leave. I was staring up at the ceiling fan and imagining I was stuck in a Tennessee Williams play, although I wasn't sure which one. The only one I could ever remember was *Cat on a Hot Tin Roof*, because of Elizabeth Taylor, but I hoped that wasn't it. I didn't want to ever have to call another man Big Daddy.

The fan was spinning and as the shadows passed over the white ceiling I let my eyes unfocus until all of it looked like a universe being born or a planet unraveling, some creation or catastrophe depending on which way gravity was going and at what end you were standing. So instead of Elizabeth Taylor I thought about stars and how little I knew about them, and how if I was an explorer and I had to sail a boat across the ocean without radar or a talking electronic compass I'd be fucked because the only constellations I knew were the Big and Little Dipper and I always got them confused. And even though I'd probably never have to sail that boat I still wished I knew more about stars and other things. And I wished I could remember lying on the grass in my backyard as a kid with my hands locked behind my head, looking up at the night sky and dreaming. But I couldn't, because it wasn't something I'd ever done. It would have been a nice memory though. Maybe it would have helped me somehow. If I was ever in jungle combat and I was captured and tortured I could look back on it and remember that innocence and all the things that seemed possible then, and I'd know why we were here fighting and dying in this godforsaken country. It was for the children. It always is. And that knowledge would have comforted me, though it would not have been enough to dim the searing pain as the electrodes sparked on my withered testicles.

"What are you afraid of?" she asked out of nowhere.

"Torture," I said.

"What else?"

"Vampires and dinosaurs."

"What else?"

"Men with tattoos on their faces."

"Why?"

"I think they might be vampires."

"Really?"

"Yes," I said.

"Is that why you wear that cross around your neck?"

"Pretty much," I said, and it was true. It was a crucifix I'd gotten for my first communion, a silver one, so it kind of protected against werewolves too even though I wasn't scared of them anymore. I took it off only to shower or have sex, and I always did both as fast as possible, and never totally without fear.

"Are you afraid of clowns?" I said.

"No."

"Good," I meant to think, but I said it instead.

We lay there for a long time with the fan turning above us and I wanted her to hold my hand but she didn't.

"I think you should go," she said.

I didn't think so, but I didn't want to move too fast. So I left. I said goodbye though, loud enough so she could hear me. And I didn't use my cigarette voice either.

Things were getting more dangerous. The plastic lock snap on my crappy yarmulke helmet broke off on one of my rides home in the rain, and since I had no brakes I couldn't go back and pick it up. The next day at work I made my own complicated fastening contraption out of paper clips. It was brilliant. I used to watch *MacGyver* like every week when it was on. Mine was just as good as the original plastic snap except that the sharp tips of the paper clips, no matter how I bent them, always lodged themselves right up against my jugular vein so if I turned my head suddenly or at all I would have died. And it looked like I was wearing headgear. "Good for that little retarded boy. He got himself some braces!" the people in their cars said as I sailed through an intersection staring straight ahead, sweating, my heart pounding, waiting to be broadsided and decapitated at the same time. I would at least die an interesting death.

My job was also getting more dangerous. And by dangerous, I mean humiliating and depressing. One morning I came back from the bathroom to an email:

```
Hey gang! Exciting news! Due to a recent floor restructur-
ing, our team is gaining a new cubicle! It will most likely
be utilized as a conference cube or for storage, but I
thought it might be fun to have a little "cube warming"
party. I know you've all been working extremely hard, and
this will be a good chance for us to "blow off some steam"
as we welcome our newest insentient addition. Say, 10 a.m.?
Be there or be square. Or, cubed, rather!
                                        Regards,
                                        Andrew
```

Then there was a rush of responses, people saying things like, "I haven't been cubed since high school!" and "Better cubed than trapezoidal!" and "All this excitement is making me elliptical!" Everyone yukking it up in their cubicles, throwing out their best geometric one-liners, hoping for that flash of comic gold that would be forwarded to people on other teams and

floors at Panopticon and talked about for weeks afterwards, remembered at company picnics and holiday parties and remi-
nisced over at retirement send-offs until they were all eventually
fired or dead. This was the mid-level corporate anecdotal im-
mortality for which they all yearned. And when Jim Fresney, a
divorced, lonely, sallow-faced college football enthusiast and
thirteen-year Panopticon employee wrote "Will we dance the
rhombus at the cube warming?" he became a god.

After I stopped crying I saw that it was 10:17. I was late.

"Shane! There you are!"

The entire team was assembled, milling around the new cubicle with its burgundy walls and gray carpet, identical in steril-
ity and hopelessness to every other goddamn cubicle in the
entire building. All it needed was a few pictures of some ugly
kids and one of those "Success Is Defined by Those Who Suc-
ceed" posters of a guy climbing a mountain, or an unframed
Thomas Kincaid print, to personalize it completely. This truly
was a joyous occasion.

"We have treats!" Andrew said. "I've brought some fruit.
Please, help yourself."

That fruit was my only consolation. Even as I stood there,
speechless with shame and disgust, I could feel a beautiful, last-
ing memory being made. All of them, my teammates, the ugly
guy, the fat guy who was gay, Jim Fresney, the old woman with
the stringy hair, even Andrew, were standing around that cubicle
with bananas in their hands. They were all eating bananas. And
that's how I knew I would always remember them: a bunch of
fucking monkeys in their natural habitat.

As I was basking in this, Andrew cleared his throat.

"You missed my earlier speech thanking everyone," he said

to me, but loud enough so that everyone stopped their mumbled conversations and listened, "but I just wanted to take this opportunity to thank you especially Shane. I know the workload can sometimes get a little crazy—"

"Sometimes?" Jim Fresney said, and everybody laughed, "Ha ha ha, hahhh." He would never forget this day.

"Yes, that's true." Andrew was smiling. "But I just wanted you to know Shane, you're doing an amazing job on your alphabetizing."

It was the most humiliating compliment I would ever receive. And I knew then that I wanted Andrew to deliver the eulogy at my funeral, which would be as soon as I had a free moment to kill myself.

"I'm sure I speak for the whole team when I say thank you. You are very appreciated." And then he began to clap. And all those monkey motherfuckers did too. They gave me a standing ovation. Smiling, nodding their heads, their hands limply slapping their banana peels as the desperate reality of this world and my place in it came crashing through the ceiling like a fucking cartoon safe. I was a man who could be applauded for his alphabetizing. That was me, at my best. I achieved on a second grade level. Did they know I could also tie my shoes and write my name in script? Would they have been astonished?

What can a grown man say to such things? I would have to ask Andrew to drop the pretenses and pay me in pelts and flat stones that I could use to make tools and fire. Oooga boooga, me am caveman.

After the applause and my dignity had completely died, Andrew said, "All right, I know this isn't how we usually do things, and I may be jumping a little ahead of myself, but the atmosphere in this cube is really getting to me so here I go. I'd like to introduce a new quotation for Inspiration Alley."

There was a collective gasp from the team as if Andrew was a detective who'd announced that the murderer was someone nobody had even suspected, like Merv Griffin. They froze in simian anticipation, their half-eaten bananas in their hands.

"I've always found this to be particularly inspirational, and while it of course has to be approved by a majority team vote—" Here everyone smiled at each other, knowing that this was mere formality. All votes were always unanimous. They were more than just a collection of random bullshit strangers who all worked for the same giant insurance company. They were a collection of random bullshit strangers who all sat on the same floor in the same cluster of cubicles. And that kind of bond cannot be broken. "—I think it will survive the process," Andrew said, and cleared his throat again. "It's by Evelyn Underhill: 'He goes because he must, as Galahad went towards the Grail: knowing that for those who can live it, this alone is life.'"

"Ahhhh" they sighed collectively, all of them beaming. Then they ripped into another round of applause which, if it weren't empirically impossible, might have cheapened the ovation I'd gotten.

"I think I can speak for all of us when I say that this belongs in Inspiration Alley," some guy in glasses and a yellow polo shirt said. I think his name was Mitch. Everyone nodded and kept their smiles pasted, but I could see they were a little disappointed that Mitch had managed to kiss ass first. They got their faces right in afterwards though, and Andrew bent over to take it like the good boss that he was.

The cube-warming assfest ended when a phone rang obscenely loud from a nearby cubicle. Mitch bolted from the gang-bang to answer it. He literally fucking ran, nimbly making a right-angle turn into his own cube. Before he picked up though he said, loud enough for everyone to hear, "No more phone calls please, we have a winner!" Then softly, "Hello, Rob speaking, how may I help you?"

Mitch or Rob or whoever the fuck he was would go far at Panopticon. Everyone laughed that politely sincere laugh that ends in a sigh and sounds like resignation and defeat from the outside, but on the inside feels like just another day at the office. Everyone except Jim Fresney. He looked heartbroken. He wasn't the team comedian anymore. His fifteen minutes were over. They'd gone so fast. He would have to live on memories from now on.

"Well, I guess it's back to work," they said, and were thankful for the break and the bananas. I had a hard time fathoming that this wasn't all shameful and degrading for them too. This wasn't abject humiliation. This was a good day. Team. Bananas. Inspiration Alley. No more phone calls please, we have a winner, ha ha ha, hahhh. For them, this was life.

I was early for my Doug appointment so I went into a fancy restaurant down the street and pretended to wait for my wife. Rich people with their napkins in their laps were having Saturday brunch. Waiters were smiling and little kids were swinging their legs under their chairs and holding their forks in their fists. Classical music was playing softly from everywhere. It sounded like Vivaldi, though I didn't really know what Vivaldi sounded like. It was all beautiful in an unfair sort of way.

I checked my watch even though I was not wearing one, and shook my head. My imaginary wife was late.

Then, when no one was looking, I stole two saltshakers. Good ones. Glass ones. Not like the brown, ribbed, lampshade kind that I'd been reduced to grabbing from bars and chain restaurants, so stark and ugly I found them insulting. They were the tenement high-rises of saltshakers. They had no imagination, and led to drugs and poverty and dreams deferred. I still stole them but I was never happy about it, or satisfied.

But these were nice. Slender and elegant, like swans, and so high class they could have been crystal. They could have been a wedding present. There wasn't even a seam in the glass, or a screw top or anything. I had no idea how they got the salt in. Maybe grain by grain, hand-fed through the hole on top like those clipper ships in a bottle. I felt sophisticated having stolen them.

"When my wife arrives could you tell her I've gone to the dentist?" I said to the maître d' as I was leaving.

"Certainly sir," he said.

The perfect crime. I was an English jewel thief. I felt good.

"HI STINK!" Marlene shouted when I walked into the office. That's what she'd called me ever since her goddamn party. It always made her laugh out loud, the memory of me standing in her backyard being ridiculed by a mob of deaf strangers.

I was not amused. I was an English jewel thief. I was a man with a crystal saltshaker in each pocket. I was many things. But I was not Stink. And it was wrong for her to say that I was. Doug could be Bus Door Head. That was true. That was right. But not this. Not this.

"Hi Deaf!" I yelled back at her. No I didn't. I always wanted to though, and it was hard not to. It would have been easy, and wrong, but it would have felt so right until I saw the look on her face. So I didn't. And that makes me a good person.

Hi fuckhead, I signed instead, then gave her the finger.

Hi dicknose, she signed back.

Hi shitface.

Hi cocksucker.

Hi asshead.

I always ran out of real curses before she did. Then we'd both smile, overly sarcastic, and squint our eyes and bow to each other repeatedly while performing elaborate gibberish hand gestures to say that we were sorry. It was like kabuki theater. Then she'd laugh because she was only kidding, and I'd laugh too because at least I could fucking hear.

Where's Doug? I want to piss on his head. He eats my shit, I signed.

He's waiting for you in the back, and she made the universal sign with her fist up to her mouth and her tongue poking the inside of her cheek, the one that said my dick would soon be in Doug's mouth. She grabbed my sleeve as I walked past her.

I have to talk to you later.

About what?

"SSSHHHH!!!" she said as she held her finger to her lips, making the loudest plea for silence I had ever heard. It was very ironic.

"Good morning Shane!" Doug was chipper and smiling. He must not have taken the bus to work. "Let's see what we have today!"

I was reclined in the chair and he sat on his stool beside me and looked at the x-rays of my mouth, trying to show me the decay and the crumbling enamel and the roots that were going bad.

"You see that spot there? That's an old filling that's rotted, tsk tsk."

I didn't like looking at skeleton me. It made me think of brain tumors and cancers. There's never good news in those things. My white skull splayed out on that black sheet looked like the flag of a pirate ship I did not want to sail. I closed my eyes and nodded.

"I've done just about all the basic work I can do, cleaned up what I could . . ."

As he talked I could feel something inching up my thigh, and if both of his hands weren't holding on to the x-ray I would've punched him in the face or just been very quiet and sad.

"I think the next step has to be crowns. I won't lie to you, they're expensive, and it's a pretty involved procedure, but they're more permanent than the patchwork I've been doing. And you're going to need some root canal. . . ."

It felt like Mobo's guinea pig was slowly climbing out of my pocket, which was very interesting since I didn't even know he was in there. I was pretty sure he wasn't. I'd have blamed the laughing gas but Doug hadn't given me any yet.

"Like I said, it's going to be expensive, so we'll have to work something out. And, ahh, we should probably take a look at the bills you have on the books for the, ahh, other work. I think—"

It wasn't until after Ivan had rolled stiffly over my hip like he had rigor mortis or like he was being especially erotic, until after he had jumped from my pocket and I heard the shattering of glass and the scattering of tiny mice right afterwards, that I remembered my fancy saltshakers.

"*Ahhh!*" Doug sighed, so effeminate he sounded like a Southern belle swooning, and the x-ray floated to the floor. He leapt down from his stool and landed with a crunch. I sat up in the chair and turned around.

"Shit." There was glass and salt everywhere. My beautiful saltshaker. "Sorry about that Doug. It was, uh, Doug?"

He was standing rigid, his arms and legs bent awkward like he was a discarded action figure, and his eyes were watering. He took a halting step and crunched more salt under his shoe, and the tears streamed down his face.

He cried out like a wounded buffalo and ran hunchbacked out of the room, lifting his legs in a cruel impersonation of a retarded Heisman Trophy winner. I heard the door of his office slam, and then I was alone.

This is what it had come to. I already had salt all over me from the night before when I'd fallen asleep with five shakers in my pockets. Now one of my fancy new ones was busted and there was salt all over the floor, and Doug was crying. What the fuck was going on.

"YOU SMELL LIKE FOOD!" Marlene shouted when she walked in.

Thank you. Where's the sweeper? I had managed to kick the glass into a small pile but the salt was still everywhere.

What?

B-r-o-o-m, I spelled out with my hand.

I'll get it. What happened?

One of my saltshakers broke and Doug started crying.

What are you talking about?

I don't know.

Why did you bring a saltshaker to a dentist appointment?

I thought we could have a picnic. I don't know.

You're a weirdo.

There was a broom but no dustpan so the best I could do was sweep the salt up against the walls, which was as much as I would've done anyway.

I have to tell you something, Marlene signed, just as I was finishing up.

What. I was demoralized from sweeping the salt and from all that I had lost.

You can't tell anyone or I'll get in trouble.

I don't care about anything.

Promise you won't tell!

Fine. I promise.

She looked over her shoulder and put her finger to her lips, even though I wasn't talking.

I cheated on my husband again.

You always cheat on your husband.

No, but bad. Bad. I slept with—and she jerked her thumb over her shoulder.

Jesus Christ.

No, I signed.

I did!

You fucked Doug?

Yes.

I wanted to beat myself into a coma with the broomstick.

No!

I did. It's bad.

I was bent over gagging, leaning on the broom so I wouldn't fall down, hoping I would die soon. I could not live in a world where Doug could fuck anyone, never mind deaf Marlene.

Stop it! She thought I was kidding, that my dry heaving was

just part of my usual over-exaggerated sign language pantomime. She couldn't hear the strained hacking in my throat, the
gurgle as I reached for bile, for anything.

Why? Why did you do it? I signed.

*I don't know! It was after my party when everyone went home. I was
drunk!*

I was shaking my head and holding my stomach.

*It was a mistake. We said we wouldn't do it again, but then we did.
This morning.* And her eyes shifted involuntarily towards the
dentist chair. The one I had just been sitting in.

"Aaaagh!" I was coughing up internal organs. I needed to set
myself on fire. I'd have to throw out these clothes and run home
naked, take a scalding hot shower and scrub my skin until it
bled, call my mother and tell her to fuck off, then start a heroin
addiction.

I'll tell you another secret—

No!

He likes anal sex.

No! You fucked him in the ass?

No! and she laughed.

I held up my hands in surrender. The details were too horrible to imagine. I knew then, and it was true, that I would be
haunted by this conversation for the rest of my life.

Why? Why did you do it?

I told you, I was drunk!

I'm drunk all the time! I never fucked Doug!

She laughed but I was serious. Disgusted and serious.

It was good! I liked it.

And there it was. Sex with Doug was good. Doug fucked like
a champ. If I tried to reconcile that fact with what I knew of him,

my head would explode. The universe is based on a certain set of laws, and Doug having sex with a woman—and being good at it—invalidated them all. Dr. Douglas Weinhardt was not a sex god. He was crying in his office because a broken saltshaker had scared him. I prayed for total amnesia.

But it's bad. My husband knows. He found the sheets.

The sheets? Oh jesus god.

He doesn't know it's Doug but he knows it's someone. I told him I got sick but he didn't believe me. I don't know what he's going to do. I need your help. I—

She looked up and so did I and there was the lumpy, hangdog figure of Doug in the doorway, his limp curls smashed to his forehead, his eyes red, the skin around them pummeled nearly purple. Clearly, this was a man who knew how to fuck.

Marlene waved away our conversation and scurried out of the room. Doug stayed in the doorway.

I cleared my throat, hoping it would clear my head of Doug and Marlene on the chair, the chair where I'd been reclined, resting my head on the cushion where Doug's bare ass had been just an hour earlier, the side of my face pressed on the same funked, slippery surface. It did not work.

"I'm, uhm, sorry about the glass. I was just—"

"It's all right Shane," he said, his voice shaking. "I feel as if I owe you an explanation."

"No, I should just go."

"No, please. I need to say this." He put his hand to his forehead, his palm facing out, his wrist bent and resting against his sweat-soaked hair.

"I have a condition," he said, taking measured, deliberate breaths. "Certain sounds, gritting sounds, or sometimes shaking sounds, affect me. Whenever I hear sand or sugar being scattered or stepped on, or maracas—" His whole body convulsed. He hugged himself tightly and bowed his head.

Even in the midst of my own trauma and horror I forced myself to look at him carefully, trying to memorize every curve and line of his face so I'd be able to provide the police with an immediate and detailed sketch when he finally went fucking insane and started blowing people away. It was only a matter of time. Probably minutes.

He composed himself as best he could.

"When I hear these sounds I tense up, my body shuts down, my muscles freeze. I can't function properly. I just need to be by myself until it passes. I've tried everything—ginseng, iced tea—nothing can control it. It just has to work itself through." He sucked in his bottom lip and looked away. He was being so brave. "So that's that. I just wanted to explain myself. So you knew." He took another deep breath and looked at me. "I hope you'll still allow me to be your dentist."

I wanted to ask him if he'd been kicked in the head by a horse as a boy or cursed by a gypsy or just what had happened to make it all turn out like this. I wanted to rock him gently and whisper in his ear, tell him that sometimes suicide was noble and nothing to be ashamed of. Sometimes, it was the answer. And in spite of the retching it would lead to I wanted to ask him what kinds of noises Marlene made and if it was ever scary. But mostly I just wanted to go home and hide.

And when he nodded and turned and ran hunchbacked into his office again, that's exactly what I did.

* * *

It was Tuesday so I knocked on the door and when Bryce answered I went into total cardiac arrest.

Whenever we saw each other around the building we had an unspoken agreement to completely ignore one another and run the other way as fast as we could without seeming obvious. That was my unspoken agreement at least. I didn't want to talk to him about having sex with his wife and I was hoping he didn't want to talk to me about how I'd stopped paying rent. No good could come of any conversation we could possibly have. Even a nod hello would have been unbearable. Subtext is fine in plays or cartoons but in real life it's very uncomfortable.

But I couldn't run this time. It would have been rude. And my legs didn't seem to be working. I was rooted in fear and awkwardness. Bryce looked terrible. His eyes were raw and his face was pale and sunken. He'd obviously been crying or projectile vomiting. He didn't seem especially surprised to see me. He just stared for a long time with his mouth moving slightly, his lips parting and unparting, saying nothing. It was like the time my grandfather tried to wish me a happy birthday but he couldn't get it out because he didn't have the mechanics for it anymore. I hugged him anyway. But Bryce wasn't my grandfather. If I'd hugged him it might have been weird.

All I could do was wait until he gave up. I didn't have to wait long. His head dropped and his shoulders sagged and his whole body shrunk down to half its usual size. I stepped aside and he shuffled past me on his weak little legs and went out the side door to cry behind the Dumpsters.

I stood in the doorway for a while.

When I went into the bedroom she was on the bed with her blue bathrobe tied around her, smoking a cigarette. She was on her back and the cigarette was straight up in the air like a chimney. She let the ash build into a column and then just as it was ready to topple she took the cigarette from her mouth and flicked it in the ashtray on her bedside table. It seemed unnecessarily risky, but it looked pretty cool.

I kept my clothes on and laid down beside her without saying anything. She finished her cigarette and crushed it out. Then, still lying down, she took a glass of water from the table and drank half of it, holding it six inches above her face and pouring the water into her mouth without the glass ever touching her lips. I'd never seen anyone do that besides me. When I drank lying down like that it hurt my stomach and gave me real bad gas. I was impressed with her performance, and afraid.

"What do you do when it's not Tuesday?" she asked.

There was Panopticon Insurance, my girl's bike, deaf birthday parties and all my saltshakers. I led a full, interesting, vibrant life.

"Not too much," I said.

"Outside interests are important," she said.

Why is the worst question anyone can ask. With the things you really want to know there's never an easy answer, and they're hard enough as it is. It's stupid to make them more complicated by trying to explain them, trying to reason out what never made sense in the first place and probably wasn't supposed to. But I couldn't help it.

"What about Bryce," I said.

She took her glass of water from the table again and drank until it was empty, gulping it down. Her throat rolled like the ocean. After she put the glass down she said, "Bryce is never happier than when he's bowling. He's always been that way."

"So it's always been like it is now?" I said.

"No. Not like now."

Good. I wanted to be brave.

"What's different?" I said.

Really I wanted her to be brave first.

"He used to take his bowling ball with him."

"Huh?"

"It's still in the closet. He hasn't touched it in months."

I looked at her and she turned her head to look at me. I could not read her face. Then she untied her robe and let it fall around her.

I didn't really want to know anyway.

So we had some sex, but slower than usual, on her open blue robe. And it was all right.

"I want to go skydiving by the time I'm thirty, and I need to learn how to play golf. I want to be through leasing by then too. From a financial standpoint it just doesn't make sense not to own."

Gwen had been talking about her life checklist and how it was important to set goals. She kept stressing the words *important* and *goals*, repeating the same goddamn thing over and over again. The way she was talking I knew that it wasn't so much about her checklist as it was the absence of mine. I nodded and listened and never once acknowledged the obvious direction of the conversation, and this made her try even harder to subtly bring it up. It was like watching a hamster in a wheel, all that tireless futility.

So far, things had pretty much gone according to schedule for her. She went to Europe for a month after college with two friends and met a *ton* of interesting people and took lots of pictures. She passed the real estate licensing exam even though she had no intention of ever becoming a real estate agent. She taught herself to speak passable Italian, and learned the fundamentals of the stock market and retirement planning. I knew without asking that she'd lost her virginity the night of her senior prom. Good for her. She had a plan and she was sticking to it. Where I fit in though, I was not sure.

Sometimes I thought she was trying to change me, save me, rehabilitate or recycle me, whatever word people use when they want to make someone else into something that other person doesn't really want to be. Maybe I was her good deed or her test case, or maybe she just wanted control. I never understand what motivates people to take such an active interest in someone else.

Sometimes I thought I was a number and a story, some background filler so that when she met her professional and romantic soul mate she could say she'd "done the dating scene" and settle down without any of the reservations she never had to begin with.

Sometimes I thought she might honestly like me, which was so ridiculous it almost could have been true. Empirically speaking, she really couldn't: we hardly talked, she knew almost nothing about me besides my first name, and I was drunk every time she saw me. But you can never tell with these things. People get stupid and delusional, sometimes on purpose. They want to make obvious mistakes. It's an easy way to turn a casual nothing of a relationship into some tragic half-assed epic, an excuse to use words like *love* and *loss* and get melodramatic about the life you wish you were leading. It's the poor man's *English Patient* starring somebody you never really cared about anyway.

Whatever it was I didn't want to know. If I didn't know I couldn't be blamed when it ended. And it would be ending soon.

"I know it's been hard lately with both of us working, you trying to go perm, me taking that automotive repair class at the community college, but I think it's important that we make time for each other. That should be one of our goals."

"Yeah," I said.

We were in one of those restaurant/bars where people I don't like go after work to unwind. The guys had their ties loosened and some had their sleeves rolled up and the girls were using their weak drinks as an excuse to act flirty. Everyone was too loud and there was always someone, somewhere, laughing. The top shelf bottles behind the bar were lit up with a depressingly ethereal blue neon light that looked like some douche bag's idea of deep sea diving or heaven, and the dude at the door who checked my ID was wearing a tight black T-shirt and called me "Chiefy."

If I was ever going to be assassinated this was where it would go down. One of these young professionals in a French blue button-down from the fucking *Men's Wearhouse* would lurch out of the crowd and shout "Oswald!" for no apparent reason and plug me in the gut. Everyone would gasp and scatter, but no one would cradle me in their arms as I died.

"You know, for all the time we've known each other I still haven't figured you out."

"Huh?"

"I don't think you're shy, but you can be really quiet some-times. It's hard to tell what you're thinking."

"Yeah," I said.

Or I'd be sitting in a wooden booth over by the window and a sniper's bullet would shatter the glass and simultaneously blow out the back of my head as I waited for my appetizers.

"Would you say you're introspective?"

"I'd say I'm self-absorbed."

"Hah hah, hmmm, then how are you such a good listener?"

I've been accused of that all my life. It's like someone who prays every night saying God's a good listener. Just because you're talking to us doesn't mean we're listening. With me and God, you never really know.

I held up my hand and showed her my two fingers crossed, like I was making a promise I knew that I would break.

"What's that?"

"That's me and God," I said.

She was dumbfounded. I was getting pretty drunk.

"Half the time I don't even know what you're talking about."

"Yeah," I said.

"I bet you think that's pretty mysterious."

"Sure."

"And I suppose you think that's pretty sexy." She stepped closer to me like we were going to dance.

"Yeah."

"David Copperfield's mysterious. I wouldn't say he's sexy."

I didn't say anything.

"Sexy and 'I got my name from a Dickens novel' don't really go together. I mean, there aren't any underwear models named Oliver Twist. No pun intended! Hah hah hah, hmmm."

She'd given up on me ever playing witty sitcom couple with her, so she'd started taking on both parts herself, feeding herself lines and then driving them home for canned laughs. Watching someone banter with themselves is fucking creepy. I felt like Howdy Doody.

"Even if you were a Dickens character, I'd still think you were sexy," she said, and batted her eyelashes like she was epileptic.

That kind of inane horseshit line was usually the preface to her ripping my shirt at the collar and pulling it down into a tube top, exposing my delicate, milky shoulders and pinning my arms at my sides. Then she'd rape and fuck me until I was a limp body ready to be flung into a mass grave.

But we were in public, surrounded by people in business clothes. I figured I was safe. But then she was biting her bottom lip and squinting her eyes like she was considering it, like maybe she'd yank me into the bathroom and brutalize me in a filthy stall. Oh jesus no.

"Gwendolyn? Omigod! How are you!"

There was a girl with shoulder-length brown hair and lipstick the color of weak coffee standing beside us. She had a pinched nose and her face was too big for her head.

"Julie! I haven't seen you since Shari's birthday! How have you been?"

"Busy enough for three people. I need to go schizo just to lead my life, hah hah, hmmm."

"Some things never change!" Gwen said.

"What about you? Are you still at Panopticon?"

"Five days a week! Hah hah hah, hmmm."

"Hah hah, hmmm—Oh, have you met Chad? Chad, this is Gwendolyn. We played rugby together in college."

"Please, call me Gwen. Only my grandmother calls me Gwendolyn."

Chad was tall. His hair was parted on the side. He'd recently had a haircut. He had broad shoulders and cuff links. He probably played lacrosse at school. Everyone in this bar was a college athlete except me.

"This is Shane," Gwen said, and I had to shake hands with these strangers and listen to Gwen tell them that I worked at Panopticon too and then not correct Julie when she assumed that was where we met. Then the two of them talked about people I didn't know and would hopefully never meet. Chad kept looking at me like he wanted to have a guy talk about sports or the market. I wanted to interrupt and say, "I'm just a temp at Panopticon you know," or "I'm a good alphabetizer." I wanted to ask Chad if he'd loan me $300 and help me carry home all the saltshakers I planned to steal from this place tonight. But I didn't. I wanted to call him Chip by mistake, but I didn't do that either.

"So nice to meet you Shane," Chad and Julie said as they were leaving.

"Sure," I said.

"Running into Julie, that's so funny!" Gwen said.

"Yeah," I said. "Why don't you tell your goddamn grandmother to call you Gwen instead of Gwendolyn?"

"What do you mean?"

"You said she's the only one who ever calls you Gwendolyn. Tell her to call you Gwen."

"Shane, what are you talking about? Both of my grandmothers died before I was born."

I never wanted to see her again.

"Anyway you always make me talk about myself. Let's talk about you instead."

"What do you want to know?"

"I don't know. Just tell me something."

"Okay. When I was seven years old I thought I was a super-hero. My name, was Leaf Man. . . ." And I told her that lie of a Leaf Man story. It wasn't a total lie actually. I really did have the GI Joe underoos and the cape made out of St. Patrick's Day napkins. But I always knew I wasn't a superhero, and I never jumped out of any trees. I thought about it, but I was too scared. I knew I'd get hurt real bad. Those poems about the fearless-ness of children are fucking bullshit.

"Oh my *god!* That's so you! You must have been hilarious as a little kid!" she said, laughing.

"Yeah."

"Taped together St. Patrick's Day napkins? Hah hah hah, hmmm."

I wanted her to pay the check so I could get out of there. Once we were outside I was going to say my stomach hurt and that I would soon have explosive diarrhea, then I'd go home and never return her calls. Maybe I'd write her a letter saying that I'd left town because of a family emergency that I couldn't really ex-plain, but that I would always remember what a special and pro-fessional person she was and cherish our time together. Or maybe I wouldn't write her at all. I just wanted to get out of there.

"I feel like we're really connecting again," she said.

"Yeah."

"Why don't you tell me something else?"

"Like what?" I didn't have any more stock footage in the archives to show her. One made up story is usually enough.

"Why don't you tell me how much you like me?"

Jesus.

"*Like* is such a strong word," I said, genuinely smiling.

"You *bastard!*" she said, and kept her mouth open, mock horrified. Then she came at me pretending to be angry, thinking she was playing along. And she was playing along, just not in the way she believed.

This was our final act together, since I planned on never seeing her again. This was it. But I wanted it to have a happy ending, even if it was somewhat mysterious and abrupt. I wanted to leave her with nothing but sweet memories of our sham relationship, to feel good about all the time we'd wasted together. I don't care if it's founded on lies and misconceptions, I like to be remembered fondly. I was feeling so magnanimous just then I would have even bantered with her maybe, if she'd bought me another drink or five. But then she started tickling me instead.

I have never reacted well to tickling. I squeal like a little girl and fall to the ground and curl up in the fetal position to protect myself. There's nothing I can do about it. It just happens. The tickling years, from kindergarten through early high school, when there's a chance you'll be tickled at random, for no reason whatsoever, were for me a season in hell. But once you reach a certain age it doesn't matter anymore. You just don't expect to ever get tickled again. It's like pissing your pants or crying. You assume those days are finally behind you. But they never really are.

And there I was, twenty-eight years old, being tickled in a crowded bar surrounded by young professionals. And God wept for the world that he had made.

Luckily Gwen didn't tickle like most people. Gwen tickled with her fists.

Ugh. Ugh. She jabbed me twice in the ribs before I even knew what was happening.

"You *think* so? You *think* so?" she said, rabidly playful, catching me once in each kidney. And then we were street fighting. I had the height advantage but the close crowd negated my long reach, so I tried to get in tight and tie up her arms, grapple with her until a bouncer separated us or threw us out or clubbed me in the back of the head and killed me. But she was too quick and slippery. I couldn't get a hold. And there was no one coming to save me.

She caught me with a left hook to the gut that sent me stumbling back, my legs wobbling. Wobbling from the alcohol, I'd like to tell myself, and often do. As I reeled I fell into the rounded back of a fat guy who had just bent over laughing at something one of his buddies said, and that sent me staggering towards Gwen like the skinny kid on the playground who's getting tossed by the circle of bullies, helpless momentum the only thing keeping him on his feet. Unfortunately Gwen had come forward for the knockout, so when that fat guy pitched me I stumbled face first into her solid linebacker's shoulder. How I stayed up I'll never know. There was a flash of black in my eyes and my head swerved, and I saw the headlights of oncoming traffic even though I wasn't in a car. There was a moment of perfect silence like just after diving into a pool. Then I felt the heat in my hands.

"Bathroom," I mumbled as I broke past her, weaving through the crowd with my hand over my mouth like I was yawning for a really long time, pinching my nose as I tried to catch the blood in my mouth. It was hot on my tongue and I almost gagged. It wasn't too far from blowing your nose right into your mouth. Maybe it was worse. There was nothing else I could do.

At least the bathroom was empty. I spit it all into the sink and hacked and coughed and washed my face as best I could. I didn't know if I was supposed to tilt my head back or keep it forward. One way the blood seeps into your brain and you get retarded and the other it goes into your lungs and you can't breathe. But I forgot which was which so I did both, wrenching my head back and forth every five seconds trying to keep the blood swishing somewhere in the middle, in a neutral canal, slowly becoming a partially retarded asthmatic. I was ripping up my face with those coarse, gritty recycled hand towels, soaking them red quicker than I could grab them and stashing them in the garbage or dropping them on the floor. I felt miserable.

I grabbed a stack of towels and went into the stall and stood leaning against the door like a junkie. I would've slept on the toilet but I was afraid I'd slip into a coma. I heard the door open and I listened as two guys stood at the urinals, talking and pissing. And then the two motherfuckers were at the sink making jokes about all the bloody towels.

"Dude, looks like somebody's on the rag!"

"It's that time of the month bro!"

Then they high-fived.

Hours passed. Days. The blood finally slowed and hardened in my nose, crusted over my brain and lungs. I would wear short pants and pull my tube socks up to my knees, carry a pinwheel around with me and an inhaler. Things would be different.

Gwen was at a window booth when I got back. There was a full beer waiting for me. "Are you okay?" she said delicately.

My nose was red and swollen and my head was pounding.

I had made up my mind in the bathroom to sucker punch her. Lean over the table and *pop* right on the bridge of the nose.

That would almost make us even. Looking at her though I wasn't sure if in my weakened and bloodless condition one shot would be enough to put her down. And one shot was all I was getting before she started throwing back. If she punched me out in front of this crowd that would be it. I'd have to leave town. I'd have to leave the country. Move to France and start over. I've never had much pride, but still.

"Shane?"

Just let me get a few beers into me, and a steak. Get some strength back. Then we'll see how tough you are sister. Realistically though, it could have gone either way. And if there's one thing my father taught me it's that if you're going to get into a fight with a girl you better make goddamn sure you're going to win you little faggot.

"Are you all right?"

I prayed that the sniper had me in the crosshairs. Hurry up and take the shot.

"Shane? Talk to me."

Please, God, somebody, take the fucking shot.

Chapter 6

I came in Monday morning to this:

This is the hardest email I've ever had to write. I just received word that Martha Wolsey, our beloved co-worker, passed away last night from a massive heart attack. She was taken in her sleep. Martha was a dedicated, caring individual who was never without a smile, and I can honestly say that she was the most gifted typist I have ever seen. She is survived by her husband, Vern.

Because of all that Martha meant to us here at Panopticon, I have received special permission for the entire team to attend funeral services at 2 P.M. Friday. This will be a paid leave of up to three hours and will not count towards personal or vacation time. I will distribute directions to the funeral home when they become available, and I would like to encourage car-pooling if at all possible. In the meantime, please take a moment to remember Martha

```
in whatever way you feel appropriate: religiously, spiri-
tually, silently, or professionally. She will be missed.
                    Regards,

                    Andrew
p.s. All rush word processing jobs will go directly to
Brenda Norris until further notice.
```

I had no idea who the fuck Martha was, but from disinterest-
edly eavesdropping on the somber, choked up remembrances
of everyone around me I deduced that she was the morbidly
obese woman who sat a few rows over and handled all the
emergency data entry jobs. No one filled in the fields of a data-
base with updated names and addresses faster than Martha. No
one.

She was a large woman, one who took "business casual" to
mean beige or black stretch pants and loose-necked T-shirts
with bead and sequin designs stitched on the front. Usually
flowers, or sailboats. She did her monotonous typing with a certain flair, altering the tempo of her keystrokes like a small town
high school band conductor, hitting the *Enter* key harder than
the rest to punctuate the end of every phrase. If anyone had ever
made data entry an art form—and they had not—it would have
been Martha.

So she was dead. A pallor of grief-stricken sluggishness and
lamentation descended over the cubicles. It wasn't really palpa-
ble at all, but everyone did their best. Brenda Norris must have
been pissed about all that extra work. Out of respect for the
dead and for the living, I hoped they wouldn't approach me
about applying for Martha's job.

I slept in the bathroom and played with my paper clip sculptures, trying to go on as best I could. The only break in the day came when Karal made his lurching rounds, hacking up the plants with his pruning shears.

"Hi," he said, standing in my cubicle, his eyes rolling back in his head.

"Hey Karal. How's it going?"

"I'm here for the plants."

"Yeah, I don't have any yet. I'm still waiting for the paperwork to go through."

"I like football," he said.

"Oh yeah? Who's your team?"

"I'm too old to sleep with my mother."

"I know you are Karal."

"Okay bye," he said.

And I was left to consider this.

I forgot about dead Martha until Friday, when I noticed that everyone was wearing black Dockers instead of khaki and nobody took lunch because they were getting out at two for the funeral. I was also getting out at two, but there was no way I was going to a funeral. I was going home.

As I was leaving I ran into Andrew.

"Hello Shane." He was politely subdued in a black shirt and solid gray tie. "Are you riding with us?"

"No that's okay. I'll, uh, figure something else out."

"You're included in the proceedings you know. I've made arrangements with your temp agency to credit you with the time even though you won't actually be in the office."

"Yeah, thanks."

"It's no trouble at all. Now let me give you a lift. It will give us a chance to talk."

"Uh, yeah, I was going to stop off and get some flowers first. I'll see you there though."

"Oh it's all taken care of. We had an arrangement sent over on behalf of the entire team. Come on," and he tilted his head and smiled kindly, because this was a tough time for us all.

There was no way I was getting roped into a talk with Andrew and blowing my Friday afternoon at the funeral of a fat woman I did not know. I didn't have any other plans or anything but still, the principle of it was repugnant.

"No that's all right. I'll catch up with you," I said.

Andrew untilted his head and squinted at me, obviously trying to figure out what I meant. I thought I was going to have to mouth "explosive diarrhea" and run to the bathroom holding the back of my pants, but then he took the hint.

"All right. Suit yourself," he said, kind of pissy, and walked away.

I didn't care. I was going home three hours early and getting paid for it. I would honor Martha's memory in my own special way: pitchers and pitchers of cheap beer, and many, many stolen saltshakers.

My phone was ringing but I didn't know what was happening. I was dead asleep and dreaming of a sandwich. I'd been eating it slowly and after every bite I said, "This is a good sandwich." Then I heard the phone and the dream was gone and my sandwich was lost to me forever.

I sat straight up in bed and salt slid down my bare chest and into my lap. I threw the sheet off of me and salt scattered over my carpet. That's when I realized I was naked, and that I had salt in my hair. Saturday mornings are always strange for me.

I let the phone ring like I always do. There's never anyone to talk to and even if there was I'd let them leave a message and just call them back sometime on my own terms. I don't understand people who bitch about telemarketers. You're asking people to bother you when you pick up the phone. It's like inviting a vampire into your house and then complaining because he bit you. You can't blame them. It's what they do. Just don't answer the phone goddamnit.

The phone kept ringing. It was 6:27 and I looked around for my clothes. My shirt was folded under the bed next to my shoes, but my pants were nowhere to be found. That was strange, even for a Saturday morning.

My answering machine picked up, and after the beep there came a voice:

"hel-lo-shane-are-you-there-shane-are-you-there," it said.

It wasn't human. It was like one of those robots from the old *Battlestar Galactica*, flat and toneless, breaking up every syllable without inflection.

"wake-up-shane-pick-up-the-phone."

I would have done whatever it asked.

"Hello?" I said.

"shane-did-I-wake-you-up."

"UH-m, yes?" My voice broke like I was thirteen years old.

"do-you-know-who-this-is."

"Uhm, no?" It sounded like someone from the future who was about to give me really bad news. I was petrified.

"come-on-think."

There was nothing to think about. I was still half asleep, but I was sure that I didn't know any robots. None who would be calling me anyway. I wasn't going to suddenly remember a robot I was friends with in high school whom I'd lost touch with over the years. To make things more complicated, I was naked and about to piss my bed, and I had salt in my hair.

"i-will-give-you-a-hint," the voice said without emotion. "you-are-stink."

"Marlene?" I said. My god, what had they done to her.

"ha-ha-ha-ha-ha-ha-ha-ha-ha," the robot voice laughed like a Japanimation villain, so echoing and hollow and sinister I almost went completely insane.

"i-need-your-help-it-is-a-bout-my-hus-band-i-can-not-talk-now-meet-me-on-the-wa-ter-front-at-noon-by-the-ja-pa-nese-me-mor-i-al-good-bye-stink."

It went so fast I could barely keep up or comprehend what it was saying. Then there was a dial tone.

What? Marlene? Waterfront? The Japanese? Was this the deaf version of *Mission: Impossible*? Was she a robot now? It was 6:30 in the morning, what the fuck was going on?

I fell facedown back into bed. Salt leapt from my pillow, right into my eyes.

I rode my crappy bike down to the waterfront. It was not what I thought it would be. I was expecting a wharf, gutted sharks hanging from hooks on the docks and big ships being unloaded by men who liked to get drunk and fight, then get tattoos. I thought it would at least be foggy.

But this waterfront was a park, a built-up urban renewal

promenade for families and tourists that stretched along a dirty river for a few hundred yards before giving way to busy streets and shopping centers. It was a wide strip of grass separating the downtown from the water, with trees and flowers in neat rows and homeless people passed out beside them. A raised concrete path was laid beside the river with a wrought-iron railing so you could look over and see the green-brown water lapping the sloping concrete embankment below. It was fucking disgusting, but it was a river that ran through a good-sized city so it didn't have much of a choice. Sewage pipes and assholes with empty cans of Bud Light will eventually kill us all.

All through the park there were ornate stone fountains that looked like they'd been dry for centuries, but then there were drinking fountains that were perpetually running, water bubbling up from a spout in the middle even when no one was around to drink it. It seemed like a huge waste. Even if it was being filtered and reused that was still a huge waste, and gross. But then I saw a little kid who was walking with his father run up to a fountain and put his thumb partially over the nozzle so the water came shooting out fast and far and he fucking soaked his dad. The guy was pissed and I'm sure he beat the poor kid senseless when he got him home, but then I didn't think the fountains were such a waste anymore.

Statues and monuments were thrown up reverently along the promenade, honoring the city founders and explorers and heroes in bronze and marble. And there were a few memorials to groups of people who'd gotten screwed over the years, usually by the same bronzed and marbled city founders and explorers and heroes. The Japanese memorial was a group of upright miniature Stonehenge-looking rocks about four feet tall with plaques laid into them talking about how the Japanese had been rounded up during World War II and put in camps because of the climate of fear and bullshit the government and the press had created. There were lots of poems and excerpts of speeches by important people, but I lacked the civic will to read any of it.

I was glad I walked past it though. Those kinds of nods and gestures are very fulfilling. It's like watching *Schindler's List* again, or not changing the channel during a Black History Month commercial. Or blowing fifty dollars on roulette at a reservation casino and not being mad. You get to feel like you're really participating, even if you had nothing to do with any of it in the first place. When something awful and shameful can be remembered and acknowledged and atoned for just by slapping up a few statues and plaques or playing a hand of poker, everybody wins.

I stood on the concrete walking path and leaned my bike against the railing and looked out over the dirty river. They'd spent all this money renovating the waterfront and left the water itself filthy and ruined. That was typical. Build a comfortable chair to sit in while everything around you goes to shit. You've done all you can do.

Still, it could have been worse. The water was rancid but it was still water, and moving, and you could look out across it at the spirals of highway and exit ramps on the other side. And there were bridges stretching out on either side of me. Everyone likes bridges. The tall buildings of the city were behind me and the water was in front of me. There were ways out if you knew where to find them.

I drummed my fingers on the wrought-iron railing and waited

for Marlene. Obviously, as I was writhing and crying on my bed of salt, I realized through the excruciating pain that she probably hadn't turned into a robot, and that she was probably using some deaf telephone conversion machine, one that translates speech into text. Then she'd read what I said and type her own words and the robot voice would say it for her. Obviously she wasn't a robot. But it would have been kind of cool if she was.

She showed up wearing a scarf over her frizzy hair and a pair of big round sunglasses that made her look like she was blind. I was going to make a joke about Helen Keller but that would have hit too close, her being deaf and all, and I couldn't think of a good one quick enough.

"HI STINK!" she shouted, scaring away all the pigeons that had been strutting around me. "YOU THOUGHT I WAS A ROBOT!" And she laughed.

No I didn't, I signed, and tried to mask my disappointment.

Is that your bike?

Yes, I signed.

"THAT BIKE'S FOR GIRLS!" And she laughed again, louder. A homeless man rolled over on the grass.

All right, all right. Why did you make me get out of bed? What the hell am I doing here? I signed.

I need your help.

She took off her sunglasses and there was a purple bruise curled around her right eye.

Shit.

What happened to you?

I fell, she signed, and gave a weak laugh. *Clumsy*, and she rolled her eyes.

I wanted to ask her about it, or instead just take a bat to her husband's big fucking forehead, like Russell Crowe in *L.A. Confidential*. But even as I thought it I immediately knew that I would not. And I immediately knew that it was cowardice, and that I would have to remember it differently later to keep from being ashamed. Excuses would have to be made, and I would make them to myself. I watched the dirty river pass below.

I need your help, she signed again. *I'm leaving my husband.*

Good! I signed quick and forcefully, hoping the righteousness and pantomimed anger would make up for my own lack of action. I felt like a politician. *You should leave him tonight*, I signed helpfully.

No, it's too soon. I have to make things ready.

I looked at her bruised eye.

Where will you go, your boyfriend?

No. I haven't seen him in a while. I'm tired of it.

Will you stay with Doug?

No way! You shouldn't shit where you sleep.

I almost threw up all over her.

Then what are you going to do? I signed.

I don't know. I just want to get away from everyone and be by myself. You know what I mean?

Yeah. I know.

I don't care about any of it, but when I tell my husband he's going to fucking go crazy. That's why I need you to keep this.

She reached into her pocket and handed me a folded check, signed and made out to me, for $800. That Martian from Looney Tunes was standing in the upper right-hand corner with his hands on his hips. I think his name was Marvin.

Why are you giving it to me?

When I tell him he's going to get pissed off and I'm afraid he'll steal all the money from our account. Most of it is fucking mine, so if I give it to you then he won't be able to find it.

Why don't you just take it out yourself and hide it? Put it in a safe deposit box or bury it in your backyard or something.

No, then he'll see that it's out of the account and he can trace it back to me, she signed.

Yeah but if I cash it, it will still be out of the account and he can fucking trace it to me instead.

No. . . . She thought about it for a second. *Oh yeah.*

Oh yeah, dumb ass, and I gave her back the check.

Fuck you! I have stress!

The pigeons had come back and they cooed and clucked around us. The smaller female pigeons pecked at the ground while two bigger male pigeons strutted and preened and tried to have sex with whoever would have them.

When are you going to tell him? I signed.

I don't know. Soon. I can't take it anymore. He's always yelling at me, saying I'm cheating on him and—

I looked at her.

I know, I know, she laughed. *I just want it to be done. I'm going to tell them all and get it over with. Maybe Doug will fire me and then I can sue him and be rich.*

Nice, I signed.

Okay, I have to go back to work, and she folded the check and put it back in her pocket. *Half hour is too short for lunch.*

Yeah it's bullshit. Tell Doug I said he eats my dick.

She put her sunglasses back on.

Be careful, I signed. *If you need anything, call me and talk in your stupid robot voice. And don't fall down anymore.*

Okay, she signed, and smiled crooked. In that scarf and those big sunglasses she looked like a ruined Jackie Onassis.

"BYE STINK!" she shouted as she waved and walked away.

With a flurry of dirty feathers and panic all around me, the pigeons flew away.

She'd started smoking cigarettes after sex. One, sometimes two, that I watched like egg timers out of the corner of my eye every Tuesday night as I sat up smoking too, my stomach churning. In the absence of any moaning or screaming or any sound whatsoever, without even Gwen's brutal "head on the dislocated shoulder afterwards" stabs at forced intimacy, I took whatever hint of satisfaction I could get from her. Even if participating in it myself made me sick.

I had never liked cigarettes and always thought that was a character flaw and the reason why I wasn't more popular. But here I had no choice. I coughed sometimes and dropped ashes everywhere and hoped she didn't notice.

I was watching the fan and thinking about Marlene and her black eye. I wanted to tell her about it, talk about it, get all worked up and be outraged as I told her the story so I could feel like I'd done something. But I didn't do anything, and there was nothing to say. I wasn't responsible for what had happened or for what would probably happen later, so there was no good in talking about it and dragging it out for other people to gawk at like it was some kind of sick spectacle. Less than a week and already I was using my Nuremberg defense. I was proud of myself in a sad, ugly way.

"A woman I work with died the other day," I said.

"Did you like her?"

"I didn't even know her."

"How did she die?"

"Massive heart attack."

"Was she old?"

"Not too old. But she was really fat."

"I don't like talking about death," she said.

"Nobody does."

"Bryce does," she said.

Naked and smoking a cigarette I did not want, "Bryce" was the absolute last thing I wanted to hear.

"He talks about it all the time. Mostly to himself in the bathroom or in his sleep. He swallowed a bottle of pills last month."

"Jesus," I said, but it was good.

"They were vitamins. Flintstones chewables."

I laughed and she smiled as she blew out a puff of smoke. In all the Tuesdays I'd been coming by it was the first time I'd seen her smile.

"It was a cry for help," was her officially sarcastic diagnosis.

"It was a cry for something. He must've pissed fluorescent for weeks," I said.

"Did you go to that woman's funeral?"

"Who?"

"The one who died. From your work."

"No."

"Why not?"

"I didn't even know her. It would've been more like a business lunch than a funeral anyway. People were just going because they were supposed to, for appearances or teamwork or some bullshit. I didn't want any part of it."

"You don't like false pretenses?"

"I usually do, but theirs seemed so insincere. Mostly I don't like going to the funerals of fat women I don't know."

"I would have gone. I like funerals."

"Why?"

"I like watching people, how they handle themselves. How the family reacts, how some people laugh and can't help it, how the funeral director shakes everyone's hand and looks at his watch."

"You like funerals but you don't like talking about death?"

"They're not the same thing. Funerals take all that useless talk and put it on stage. That's where you can separate people."

"Into what?"

"The ones who know they're on stage and the ones who know but don't care," she said.

"I've only been to two funerals."

"Your parents?"

"No, my parents are both alive."

"I thought everyone's parents were dead by now," she said, and drew in long from her cigarette and held it.

"Are yours?"

"No." She smiled again as she exhaled, smoke curling towards the ceiling fan and scattering.

Two smiles in one night. That was something.

"You should go," she said after her second cigarette was done.

So I left. And on the way out I wondered just what she was doing, and if it was a game whether I was even playing.

* * *

Detective Brooks opened the door.

"It's time," he said.

They led me to a small room that had a sink and a toilet but it seemed much too sinister to be called a bathroom. I would never have been able to sleep there.

Brooks handed me a reinforced plastic baggie that had a zip top.

"We need a sample," he said.

No lotion or magazine or anything.

"I can't jerk off into a plastic bag," I said. "It's Easter." I was feeling punchy and ridiculous and afraid. I was already working on my insanity defense.

"You can and you will, or we'll have the Easter Bunny come in there and do it for you," Sikes said.

"What the hell is wrong with you two? It's not Easter." Brooks was disgusted with us both again.

"I am not resisting arrest!" I said as I shut the door, but nobody thought it was funny except me.

Jerking off in that sinister little bathroom was actually kind of erotic, considering what was at stake. I think it had something to do with being so close to the holding cells and all those criminals. One night I was in a bus station bathroom in Tulsa, Oklahoma, washing my hands and under one of the doors I saw a pair of black patent-leather shoes and a pair of red Converse high tops, both in the same stall. "If it feels good, it's not gay," a hushed voice was pleading. I needed to get back on a Greyhound and quick. There even if things didn't make sense you at least never ended up jerking off in a police station.

Since I had some time to myself I finally thought about Marlene. Not like that. I just thought about her. I only knew her incidentally really. It wasn't like I'd give the eulogy at her funeral or anything. I couldn't get that sentimental. But I knew I'd miss having her around. It was like being a kid and having someone on your block move away. Not your next door neighbor or your best friend, but somebody down the street you used to play with and now the kickball teams would be uneven and it wouldn't be like how it was.

I finished up and gave Detective Sikes a warm bag of the best of me. I made sure I handed it to him.

Chapter 7

The bar down the street from my apartment was a cramped, dingy, worn out old place, always just dim enough so you could barely make out the small swarms of fruit flies that rose from wherever you'd set your drink. But it was cheap enough that you really couldn't complain about them. There were never more than four people in there at a time, and everyone always sat at the bar.

The seven-to-ten A.M. happy hour brought in a few drunk ass old men and some guys from the road crews, the ones who stand there all day leaning on the Slow and Stop signs trying not to fall down. They were never young and had never just shaved, and the ones who had hair looked like they were wearing bad toupees. Sometimes women came in, and they looked exactly like the men except their toupees were worse, but usually they didn't come in.

There was food on the menu but I never saw anyone order any. The condiments were lined up on the bar in case they did though: old half-empty glass bottles of mustard and ketchup with the dried blackened overspill creeping out from under the cap like mold, grimed pepper and saltshakers with pushed-in tin tops. I always sat near them, and when the bartender turned his back I would think about stealing one or maybe two, but then I would not. And that, that is loyalty.

It was a good place to wait out the early mornings, a good way to get used to the idea of another day. The windows were made out of a special, magic glass, like the bottoms of old Coke bottles or the stuff they use in two-way mirrors—there were principles at work that I did not understand—so the windowpanes would glow orange amber and repel the sunlight, keeping the bar dim while still letting you see outside, and you could watch the morning get bright in a garbled, distorted sort of way. It was like sitting in a cave that served beer. It was very primordial. During happy hour pitchers of Miller High Life were only three dollars apiece. And that is probably why I showed up to work piss drunk all those days.

I'd stumble into the office and go straight to the bathroom and pass out. When I woke up an hour or two later I'd still be ragged drunk or in the early stages of a debilitating hangover with permanent nerve damage in both legs. Getting back to my chair was a Greek tragedy of chemical imbalance and full-blown cerebral palsy. I'd stagger past co-workers and fall into cubicle walls and I didn't even care that I was obviously hammered and reeking of stale cigarettes and alcohol and that there were swarms of fruit flies nesting in my hair. And these people would smile at me and say, "Having fun yet?" or "Is it Friday yet?" or "Time to go home yet?" completely oblivious to my ruination, rhetorically seeking their own better times that wouldn't ever come, even when they did.

Sometimes you are left with no choice but to manufacture your own fiascos, and alcohol is an easy and legal variable to introduce. I was curious—scientifically, economically, sociologically, morally—as to whether I could function as an alphabetizer for a large insurance company even though I was too drunk to recite the alphabet without singing it. But what if I could? What if I could keep up even as my liver failed and I went blind from alcohol poisoning? What if I could excel? What would this say about capitalism? About the unyielding corporate machine? About the fate of the individual in an increasingly conformist American society? Sometimes the questions are more important than the answers, especially when you do not know what the answers are.

I didn't give a shit either way. I just couldn't take working at Panopticon Insurance anymore. Changes had to be made, but I didn't want to be the one to have to make them. I figured if I was drunk all the time I'd be even more obviously incompetent and they'd have no choice but to fire me. As bad as it was I couldn't bring myself to quit. Quitting is too proactive, and it reflects poorly on a person's character. Nobody likes a quitter. I would always rather be a victim of circumstance. And I thought if I got fired I could apply for unemployment, which I know now isn't fucking true.

But it didn't happen. Not the way I thought anyway. Nobody even noticed. Or if they did I doubt they associated my stumbling and slurred speech and snoring with raging early-morning Miller High Life binges. They probably thought I had a cold, or was really stressed out from all my alphabetizing. There are a fixed set of explanations most people apply to situations, and if one of those easy explanations doesn't fit they either push harder to make it fit or they ignore the whole goddamn thing and watch TV. That's why trial by jury is so terrifying for black men who aren't famous. That's why mediocre childhoods are a blank check to be an asshole. That's why shitty actors on crappy sitcoms are so rich and beloved. That's why so many unthinkable atrocities continue for as long as they do unchecked. Genocide. Serial incest and inbreeding. My employment at Panopticon Insurance. All so horrible they defy reason or explanation. To sensible people, it just doesn't make sense. It just can't be. Sleeping in the bathroom and getting drunk at seven A.M.? It hardly even made sense to me. But we still do the things that we do.

And yet unchecked Miller High Life abuse is not without its upside. It is the goddamn champagne of beers after all. And so I was able to stand on the eighteenth floor of the Panopticon Insurance building with my hand on my cubicle wall, my whole body swaying, my knees buckling beneath me, and immediately recognize what was wrong. It was all part of something bigger of course, something so deeply entrenched and terrible and accepted that I was never quite drunk enough to name it. But in that state I could see more of it than most people would normally allow themselves to see. And I even knew how to fix some of it. It was like what Buddhists call satori, and all I had to do was get trashed. I didn't have to meditate or anything.

The idea of cubicles was bad enough, but making people sit in them all day was just inhuman. They had to go. They were like The Hole in southern prisons or how farmers raise veal. It was like sticking a brick of cocaine up your ass and smuggling it across the border. Things were being crammed into places they were never meant to fit. And what these people did to their cubicles made it even worse. Dressing them up with trinkets and pictures, always trying to make their fabric walls look hospitable and just like home. I understood why they did it, but that didn't make it right. Lying to other people is fine and usually funny, but lying to yourself is tacky. There's nothing hospitable about

an 8' × 8' carpeted holding cell on the eighteenth floor of an insurance building, and it would be wrong to forget that. To pretend otherwise only blurs the line between work life and real
life, and that's a line that needs to be starkly and brutally en-
forced. Boundaries are fucking important.

And everyone drank too much coffee too, at the wrong times
and for the wrong reasons. They drank it when they came in
every morning to get going, and then again in the afternoon to
keep going. They ran on caffeine fumes all day and never fucking got anywhere. Then they went home spent and empty and
crashed in front of the TV every night and slept away the few
hours they had for themselves. All these motherfuckers are always talking about the best ways to manage your time. The fact
is any time spent at work not sleeping in the bathroom is wasted
time, and it's hard to sleep when you're pumped full of caffeine.
Everyone's awake for the wrong part of their lives. And by the
weekend they're too exhausted from all the frantic, useless ac-
tivity to even care, and it's only fucking two days off anyway.
Nobody has the time or the energy to do what they really want,
or to even figure out what that is. That's why everyone's so
pissed off and blowing each other away on the freeway and having sex with prostitutes all the time.

And goddamn Inspiration Alley was so grotesquely misguided it pained me to even have to acknowledge it, even more
so because nobody else did. It was the execution-style murder of
context. It was history castrated to a sound bite. It was seeing a
rainbow in the waves of an oil slick as it seeped across the ocean
drowning fish and strangling birds and believing that ecological
catastrophes had their own redeeming beauty. A world in which
it's possible for someone to associate Martin Luther King with

increased alphabetizing efficiency is a world in which none of us should ever want to live.

Whether knowing these things made me a prophet or a management consultant I wasn't sure. I think they might be the same thing now anyway. I could have tried to tell someone, tried to make them understand, but I didn't really want to. It wouldn't have helped anyway. This was a system so sick, so tainted, no good could ever come from it. Except when they had huge company-wide charity drives and raised a lot of money for the United Way. But that was offset by the humiliation of Jeans Day and having to gather around someone's cubicle to sing "Happy Birthday" in monotone and all the other ways in which a person was diminished every day until they became so small not even the United Way could save them.

Even something so seemingly right as Bring Your Daughter to Work Day in that environment was horribly, horribly wrong. Marching a sweet, innocent nine year old who likes ponies and dreaming into an 8' × 8' cubicle and telling her that if she's strong and independent she'll get to spend forty years in there slowly wasting away is an exercise in feminist misogyny. It was like a fucking Scared Straight program, a right-wing Christian conspiracy to create more stay-at-home moms. You grab a little girl by the pigtails and say, "Suzy, this is what hell looks like!" and obviously she's going to kick off her shoes and get pregnant at fifteen. And she'll keep on going for as long as the clock runs, anything to stay out of that cubicle.

If I could ovulate that's where I would've been. But I could not. But I could not.

*   *   *

The bartender at my happy hour bar was also the owner. His name was Sooj. That's what people called him anyway, what the old men mumbled to get his attention. I never saw an official document from the guy or anything. He looked Lebanese but he was born in Cleveland. His parents though were both from Lebanon.

Sooj obviously didn't like his deadbeat customers. He served their drinks like he was doing them a favor, which he probably was since he never cut them off. Even when they passed out with their head on the bar he'd let them sleep through it, then serve them again when they woke up. It was touching in a desperate sort of way.

He kept to himself as much as a bartender could. The only thing he liked to talk about was how, if someone broke into your house, you were allowed to kill them.

"It is a question of security! You must protect your family from harm!" he'd rant in his understated Cleveland accent. "It goes back to prehistoric times!"

Sometimes the old men would wake from their comas just long enough to frame the terms of debate: "What if it's not your house? What if you're just renting?" "Or house-sitting?" "What if it's a woman who's breaking in?" "What if you broke in first and no one was home, then someone else broke in after you? Are you allowed to kill them?" "What if you're asleep and—ahhh fuck it."

The result was always the same. Sooj was wise, like Solomon but shorter, and he never lost an argument.

A young guy came in once, greasy and in clothes too tight and too short to realistically be his. He looked like he'd gone to audition for the pickpocket role on *Starsky and Hutch* and then found out that it had been cancelled in the seventies. He got into it with Sooj pretty good and he seemed like he knew what he was talking about, like maybe he'd been in the situation a few times himself. He said that it depended which state you lived in—Texas you could shoot anything that wasn't already dead, Utah you had to invite them in for tea and then make them your wife, whether you were attracted to the guy or not—and even in some of the vigilante states it wasn't always justified, depending on the threat the intruder posed and other mitigating circumstances, except he called these other mitigating circumstances "other fucking shit."

Sooj listened patiently and then had one thing to say to him, one thing only: "Deadly force is authorized!" It was what he went with whenever debate had to be squashed immediately. There was nothing left to say. The pickpocket bummed a cigarette and left. The old men nodded into their drinks and I learned a lesson I had learned a thousand times before: facts and reason are nothing against a good slogan. No one can argue with a bumper sticker. Not when it's on the bartender's car.

Sitting on my stool I thought of a bumper sticker: "If Mean People Suck, Why Isn't My Dick In Your Mouth?" But I did not tell Sooj. I did not tell anyone.

Into this fascist cesspool, one Sunday morning, walked Gwen.

"Oh my god, Shane!" she said, and hit me with an open field tackle of a hug that lifted me off my stool and cracked two of my ribs. I saw her coming at the last second and braced myself. Otherwise I would've been paralyzed for life.

"How are you?" she said as she crushed me like a grape.

I could only gasp for air, and pray.

"I've been looking all over for you. You didn't return any of my calls, I hadn't seen you, I thought, well, anyway, here you . . . are," and she looked around at the dim, dirty bar with its fruit flies—who were regarding her with suspicion, just like Sooj—

and its Miller High Life, The Champagne of Beers poster that was peeling slowly and inexorably off the wall like the shifting of tectonic plates, and its old man three stools down who was sleeping soundly with his head in the crook of his elbow, passed out on the bar.

"I'm just glad you're all right," she said.

"Yeah. How are you?"

"I'm good, I'm good. But it's been hard. It's been hard for all of us."

She seemed very sad and I wasn't sure what tragedy I'd missed. Maybe a nuclear holocaust. Maybe the special glass had saved me and Sooj and the old man. I thought of all the cock-roaches that must be running around, flipping over parked cars with their brand new nuclear-mutated strength, smug and ruth-less, at last the dominant species they were always destined to be. I thought of them and I was afraid.

"You just can never be ready for something like that. It took us all by surprise."

"Yikes," I said.

"Poor Vern. They were married for twenty-seven years. At least they didn't have any children."

"Huh?"

"I heard they're talking about naming her cube the Martha Wolsey Memorial Cubicle, but it would just be used for storage and remembrances. That would be too creepy and disrespectful if someone else sat there."

"Oh yeah. Martha's dead," I said.

"I know," and she hugged me again. "I was so sorry I couldn't go to the funeral. I had a PowerPoint presentation. There were clients coming in. It couldn't be rescheduled."

"Yeah I didn't go either."

"What?" she said, pushing me out of the hug and looking in my face.

"I didn't go either."

"To the funeral?"

"Yeah."

"Why not?"

It seemed an absurd question, and it was only nine o'clock in the morning and I was already pretty drunk, so I didn't understand it at first.

"Uh, what?"

"Shane," she put both of her hands on my shoulders and squared me to her, "Why didn't you go to the funeral? Wasn't the entire team given special permission to attend?" She was talking to me slowly and enunciating her words like I was a small, retarded child. Which technically, at that point, I may have been.

"Yeah. But I went home instead."

"You what?" She was getting loud. "I can't believe you'd— why did you go home?"

"I didn't even know her."

"Yes you did!"

"No I didn't," I said calmly.

"That's not the point!" She was furious. Irrationally so, I thought. "The *entire team* was going. Do you have any idea what that means?"

I wasn't sure, and I think my vacant stare conveyed this.

"My god Shane! My god!" She shook her head and looked around for someone to second her indignation, but nobody in the bar cared. "You need to be more sensitive to these things!"

"What, like I should wear a velvet cowboy hat and start blowing guys? Maybe sing some Depeche Mode in a bus station bathroom? "Personal Jesus"? Is that what you want to hear?" I shouted, because I wanted to be irrationally angry too.

"What are you talking about?" she said.

I also was not sure.

She steadied her voice.

"All I'm saying is you need to be more sensitive to the dynamics of certain situations and relationships, professional and otherwise."

"Huh?"

She exhaled, controlling herself.

"There are certain obligations that a person has, certain responsibilities, and it's important to keep your long term goals in mind when you make decisions."

"So you're saying it was a poor business decision not to go to big fat Martha's funeral?"

"Frankly Shane? It was! And I don't care what you say about—"

"That's terrific. Very humanitarian," I said.

"—the team dynamic or me or anything else, there's no reason to insult Martha. She's dead."

"I know she's dead. I was just being honest and descriptive."

"No, you were being an asshole."

"It's not my fault they have to always be the same thing."

"Oh, you're *so* wise," she said.

"All right, what's the first thing you think of when I say Martha?"

"I think of what a good person she was, what an amazing typist—"

"Amazingly fat typist."

"All right, that's it. We're not having this conversation. You're drunk."

"So what. That doesn't mean I'm not right. Martha had a heart attack because she was overweight. That's a fact. I'm just trying to help here. There are lessons for all of us to learn. We can't let her die in vain. And I'm not drunk for your information."

"Fine. Then you have no excuse. So don't call me when you sober up."

"Okay BYE!" I shouted after her as she stormed out.

The old man never even stirred. He slept through all the shouting like the little withered angel that he was. The bar was suddenly quiet and eerie and still. The mildewed Miller High Life poster wasn't used to this kind of commotion. Neither was Sooj. He was standing with his arms folded, regarding me and the situation.

I gave him a sheepish grin and put both my hands up, hoping that he'd had a similar experience at some point and knew what I meant. Then we'd swap stories and make generalizations about women and maybe he'd give me some free beer.

Sooj put both hands on the bar and leaned forward, his dark eyes not far away from mine. "Do you own a gun?" he said.

I was fumbling with my keys at the door when Bryce stepped out of the shadows and scared the shit out of me. I didn't even know my front door had shadows. You never notice these things until after you're already fucked.

"Bryce, jesus," I said, struggling not to collapse.

"Hello Shane." He wasn't as jumpy as usual. His arms were at his sides and out a little, like he was making a conscious effort to have better posture. I didn't see a shiv in his hand but it could have been in his back pocket, or tucked in his belt behind his back like a pirate. "I need to talk to you," he said.

"Sure. Do you want to come in?" I had my key in the lock finally. I was fully prepared to open the door, leap in and then slam it on his arm as he plunged the knife after me. I would scream like that bug-eyed woman from *The Shining* and anyone watching would be humiliated for me and annoyed, but I would live.

"No. I'd rather talk here," he said.

He didn't want to get blood on the carpet. Sure. It was probably better this way. There were saltshakers everywhere, all over my bed and on the floor. I didn't want that to be the last thing I tried to explain before I died. He took a step closer to me.

"I know about you and my wife," he said.

I wish I could have seen the look on my face. It's so rare that your mouth actually drops open from being genuinely bewildered. I must have looked like a fucking cartoon.

"I . . . know, you . . . know?" I said.

"I want it to stop," he said, pushing his arms out a little further and leaning slightly forward.

"It might be too late for that," I said, shocking myself.

For about four seconds it could have gone either way. We stared at each other and I was cringing inside. A guy with that many tattoos had to know how to fight, or at least have a high threshold for pain. I would bite and scratch and pinch. I would use my nails. I would start crying and pretend to throw up and then kick him in the nuts. I was frightened and feeling faint but for those four seconds I didn't blink.

And then Bryce fell apart. He completely deflated and dropped his head and scratched the back of his neck with both hands.

"I know, I know it is," he whimpered, and I took my clenched fingers off my keys and left them hanging in the door. I would not get stabbed, not tonight. Not by Bryce at least. "Can I just tell you though?" he was pleading. "I didn't used to be like this." He locked his hands over his thinning pompadour. "I used to be in a band you know. A long time ago."

"Rockabilly?" I said.

"No, funk. We were called the Funktastics."

"I see."

"We used to play all over town." His eyes were getting glassy and I was getting impatient. "We were good too. I played bass and sang sometimes. Never enough, but sometimes. Those were great days. It was really a lot of fun. But she never came to see us play. Not once. She's the reason I quit making music. She never believed in me."

No Bryce, you never believed in yourself, is what I wanted to say, but I would've been openly laughing at him. I owed the guy over $1,000 in back rent and I was having sex with his wife. There was no need to uselessly antagonize the poor fuck. I just needed to let him get it all out, maybe give him a hug, then dead bolt my door.

"Yeah," I said.

"And I know I've got problems now, but I'm doing the best I can, you know? Everyone's got problems. It's not like I'm begging for change or robbing people or anything. I'm trying to work through it all, getting myself back. Like the guy in that movie, you know?"

"Sure," I said. I think he was talking about Sloth from *The Goonies*. If I'd had a Baby Ruth I would have given it to him.

"I see what she's doing too. I don't like it, but there's nothing

I can do anymore. We don't talk much. But I wanted you to know that I don't want this. I don't know if that counts for anything."

"Yeah," I said, because it really didn't.

"You should be careful," he said, looking me in the eye, and I wasn't sure if it was a threat or a warning or if he was just trying to teach me something about life. I hoped not. Bryce was in no position to be giving anybody advice about anything. And I think he realized this because he put his hands in his pockets and shrugged and started to walk away. He stopped after a few steps and turned around.

"I really don't think she cares," he said.

"About you?" There was no need to be that cruel but he was pissing me off. And I wanted to hear him say it.

"About anything," he said.

There comes a time in every man's life when he wakes up drunk on the toilet and begins to doubt the choices he has made. And when that time comes at least twice a day, every day, something needs to be done.

But what? And how? These are hard, entirely unspecific questions. And apathy has its own slow momentum. It doesn't like to be disturbed.

It had reached the point where I could hardly sleep anymore. So I sat on the toilet and read whatever crumpled newspaper pages people left lying around. It was usually the business section. Things were not looking good. I was concerned about the Fed's position on interest rates for reasons I could not fully explain. Sometimes I sifted through the scraps of paper in my wallet, a few old receipts and this clipping my mother had given me in high school from *Reader's Digest*. Points to Ponder. One of them was by Erma Bombeck. They were all needlessly depressing.

I sat at my desk and made sculptures out of paperclips. I bent them at strange angles and made them stand up. I linked them into chains that were conceptual and open to interpretation. I did other things that were avant-garde and very interesting. Sometimes I went for walks around the floor with a stack of papers in my hand, pretending to be going somewhere. But I was not. Sometimes I would stand very still and listen to the hum of the air vents, and when someone saw me I would nod and smile and walk away.

These were the longest days of my life, and I was wasting them. That is always a sad thing to know. Everyone else was wasting them too, but that only made it a little easier to take.

Sometimes I thought about things, what to do about Bryce and his wife or if I should do anything, or sometimes about Marlene and her black eye and how I wouldn't be going back to Doug's office anymore. I tried not to think about any of it too much. I was hoping it would all just work itself out. One day I thought of a bumper sticker: "The world is your oyster, but you are allergic to shellfish." That was too good to be a bumper sticker, and too long probably. Maybe it could be in a fortune cookie.

I sat there as the fabric walls of my cubicle, and all the cubicles, and all the walls of the building closed around me like one big malevolent cocoon. Maybe soon I would emerge a beautiful butterfly. Or maybe some guy out cutting his grass would mistake me for a nest of gypsy moths and set me on fire to save his trees. I wouldn't blame him. It's so hard to tell the difference these days. You have to really be paying attention.

"Shane, can I see you for a moment?" Andrew said, standing

in the open side of my cubicle. He was gravely polite.

Finally.

I staggered after him and fell into a springback chair as he shut the door to one of the private conference rooms. My eyes were so bloodshot I looked rabid. I could have been a POW.

Andrew sighed softly.

"Shane, let me just start by saying that your work for us here has always been impeccable. There have never been any questions about your abilities as an alphabetizer."

I began to weep.

"You've displayed a lot of the qualities we look for in prospective hires, but in the end we decided that you'd probably be a better fit at another company. We're going to have to let you go," he said.

"Yeah," I said, and started to get up.

"I really shouldn't comment on this any further, but I feel as if I have to," Andrew said, lowering his voice even though I could already hardly fucking hear him. I sat back down again. "This company, and the entire insurance industry as a whole, isn't just about numbers and quotas and how many forms you can alphabetize in a day. It's about people. It's about integrity and compassion. It's about what makes us human beings. I've heard about your 'imitations' of Carl as you make your way back from the bathroom, mocking his walk, his disability. I don't know who you thought you were entertaining, but it's no one on this floor. No one in this entire company. Carl may not technically be affiliated with Panopticon, but he's still a valued member of our team. The human team. And he's a veteran. He sacrificed his body so that we could enjoy the freedoms we have today. He deserves not only your respect, but your undying gratitude."

Andrew was gallant and flushed and trembling. He would tell people of this speech for years, and he would be proud of himself. And rightfully so. He had done his duty, just like Karal.

A 600-year-old security guard watched me as I packed up my paper clip sculptures and my miniature nooses, his hand quivering over his holstered gun. I touched the door of the men's room as I passed. It was like leaving home to go to college.

"Hey Shane! TGIF!" Mitch said as he stepped out of the elevator and I stepped in. He didn't know I'd just been fired. Andrew would send out an email, call a team meeting and explain. They would shake their heads and denounce me. I would be condemned and vilified. Rumors would spread. No one would defend me, not even Mitch and my other teammates, not even for my miraculous alphabetizing.

In the passion play that my life had not nearly become, this was my crucifixion: getting fired from a job I did not want for being unpatriotic. This was my Good Friday. I would descend into a Miller High Life–soaked hell for the rest of the weekend before rising on the third day to an ad in the Sunday classifieds:

> Two-month sleep study. Participant must be able to pass out on toilets for up to one hour at a time. Nudity optional. Data will be used to determine the crippling effects of modern life on the physical and psychological health of the individual. Generous compensation package including full health benefits, open bar, 3.4 million dollar stipend, worldwide fame and scientific immortality. Only serious applicants need apply. We are an equal opportunity employer.

Redemption is important. And it's fun to be Christ-like, when the circumstances fit.

∴ part two

Chapter 8

When I woke up that Sunday after getting fired Marlene was dead. I was in a salty bed and two detectives were staring down at me. Three hours later I was jerking off in a police station bathroom. It was not the resurrection I'd been hoping for.

When they let me go I went straight back to my apartment. My phone was ringing as I walked in the door. Even though I hadn't spoken to her in a long time and she didn't have my number I hoped it was my mom. It probably wasn't but I picked up anyway.

"Momma?" I said.

"IS THIS SHANE?" a man shouted, so loud and atonal and nasal it made me wince.

"Yes."

"YOU KILLED MY WIFE!"

It was either the worst telemarketer in the world or Marlene's husband.

"No I didn't," I said.

"YOU'RE GOING TO PAY FOR WHAT YOU DID YOU SON OF A BITCH!"

"Stop shouting, I can't understand you. Use the robot voice," I said. It was hard to understand him. He talked much deafer than Marlene.

"FUCK YOU!" he wailed.

"What?"

Then there was a pause.

"you-killed-my-wife-you-mo-ther-fuck-er," the robot voice said slowly, and I was back on *Battlestar Galactica*.

"I did not."

"i-have-proof."

I knew it couldn't have been true, but in that flat, dispassionate, mechanical monotone, it was still quite chilling.

"she-tried-to-end-the-af-fair-and-you-would-not-let-her."

"What? I didn't have an affair with her."

"you-are-a-li-ar."

"Listen, I'm sorry Marlene's gone but I had nothing to do with her, uh, passing."

"you-bet-ter-hope-the-po-lice-get-to-you-be-fore-i-do."

"I just came from the police station. They asked me some questions and told me to go home." I didn't mention that they'd also told me not to leave town or I'd be the star of a statewide shoot-on-sight manhunt. That I kept to myself.

"what-they-let-you-go."

"Yeah, see? I'm innocent."

"you-killed-my-wife."

"I didn't kill anybody."

"I-found-her-blee-ding-in-the-bath-room-i-know-what-you-did."

"I didn't do anything, but I told the police about you shit-head."

"what-are-you-talk-ing-a-bout."

"That black eye you gave her? Yeah you're a real tough guy beating up on your wife."

And I was a real tough guy telling him so over the phone as I checked my door to make sure it was locked.

"you-fuck-ing-li-ar."

"Nice try framing me for it though. Too bad it didn't work out for you. I bet you'll be real popular in those prison showers."

"YOU MOTHERFUCKER! I'LL KILL YOU—"

I hung up and hoped he wouldn't call back and prayed he didn't know where I lived. My ears were ringing and I still had the shakes from the creepy robot voice.

So that was his angle. He'd already gone to the police, trying to set me up. His "proof" was probably that picture I'd drawn of her with the horse teeth sitting on a pile of garbage. Even with the crooked cops that wouldn't be enough. I was safe.

Still, he sounded pretty sure of himself. It was hard to really judge, since he talked like a robot most of the time, but he seemed like he believed what he was saying. He was already preparing for the polygraph. He was a crafty deaf man.

So Marlene had died in the bathroom, just like Elvis. That was a shame. I hadn't even known how it happened. I'd never even asked the police. Fuck. Did that make it seem like I already knew? Was that suspicious? But I was in shock, how could anyone expect me to be thinking clearly? I was anguished. I was in no condition to ask thoughtful, obvious questions. But I could crack jokes before jerking off into a plastic bag. That I could easily do. It wouldn't look good to a jury. I'd convict me in a heartbeat, then be home in time to watch the ripped-from-the-headlines TV movie. I would be played by a pretty boy actor who was looking to showcase his gritty, serial killer side. The Greyhound Strangler they'd call me. Fuck.

I went down to the bar to at least get my alibi straight. There was an unlit neon-lettered sign over the door that I made sure I remembered: The Mickeypot Tavern. So that's what it was called. I liked it better when it was just the place with the seven-to-ten A.M. happy hour.

I sat at the bar and paid regular price for a pitcher of Miller High Life. Five dollars was a lot to spend, but I needed something familiar, something I could trust to sicken me in that old reliable way. Projectile vomiting can be very reassuring sometimes. And I needed to talk to Sooj. I had to make sure he'd vouch for me. I knew I hadn't done anything, but the police and the robot voice had gotten me pretty spooked. Not spooked enough to where I was doubting myself, but pretty spooked.

Still, asking a strange man from Cleveland to please, please keep you out of prison isn't as straightforward as it seems. Etiquette is important. And there were other considerations, the biggest one being that I wasn't sure I was even in here the night Marlene died. I thought I was. I didn't know where else I could've been besides here or passed out in my bed. But what if I wasn't? Would that make me seem even more suspicious, like I was shopping for an alibi wherever I could get it? From some pissed off bartender whose parents weren't even from this country? How would Sooj play on the witness stand, shouting,

"Deadly force is authorized!" during the cross-examination? Christ.

All I had in my defense right now was my good word and a bag of sperm. I was nobody, and who knows what they do with DNA testing? It can be faked and tampered with just like anything else. And how the fuck would anyone know? Are you a scientist? Are you?

No, I needed Sooj. Sooj was the best I could do. Christ.

But how do you ask someone for an alibi? What are you supposed to say?

"Last night was busy, huh?" I said, smiling and wishing I had a microphone taped to my balls so I could record his answer and not go to jail.

Sooj looked at me with utter contempt, like I was the biggest asshole in the world, then went back to staring at his hands.

So that didn't work. I would need a new strategy. And as I drank my pitcher I tried to think of one. But I could not. Midway through my second pitcher I came up with a few ideas. They were convoluted and hilarious, and most of them involved me wearing disguises and running around to funny music like on *Benny Hill*, but I didn't have the courage to try them. Not yet. By my third pitcher I had forgotten all about them and I didn't even care.

I didn't kill Marlene. The whole thing was ridiculous. I'd blacked out from alcohol plenty of times before. Some of those times I'd done things with ugly women that I never would have otherwise done. Sometimes I'd pissed places I probably shouldn't have pissed. Sometimes I did other things that were gross and sad. But I'd never blacked out and murdered anyone before. You'd have to be really religious to do something like that. Or famous and on designer drugs at least.

Obviously I wouldn't be sent to prison for a crime I didn't commit. That happened to the fucking A-Team, not me. This would all be straightened out tomorrow somehow. I was confident my name would be cleared. Maybe I could sue those cops for making me jerk off. Fuckers. I'd like to see them try it now. Yeah, fucking perverts. I'd sue them, then after the trial I'd fight them on the steps of the courthouse in front of all the reporters and I'd make *them* jerk off *all over each other*. Two disgraced cops whacking each other off. People would be taking pictures and everything. Yeah.

There were two old men at the bar, one on either side of me. No one was talking. We were all just sitting with ourselves and our beer.

"Why are dogs better than women?" the old man to my left said suddenly, then coughed phlegm into a filthy handkerchief for about twenty minutes until it was heavy and full. Sooj glared at him from behind the bar, his arms folded, saying nothing. I didn't say anything either because I wanted Sooj to like me, but I was very curious. The old man had a few strands of white hair that stood up on his ancient head, and they waved like withered grain as he shook with coughing. The other old man on my right had his eyes closed and he swayed on his stool like a dreidel right before it spins out. Chanukah would be ending soon. I hoped he wouldn't crack his head when he landed on the floor.

Finally the coughing man pulled the sopping wet rag from his face.

"You can give them a bone and you don't have to call them the next day!" he said, and laughed phlegm and filth into his handkerchief.

It was by far the funniest thing I'd ever heard in my entire life, but Sooj wasn't laughing so I bit my cheek hard and tried to keep a straight face. The other old man beside me wasn't doing anything but getting ready to fall down. I don't even think he was conscious. I was going to tell my sex with a three year old joke, to show Sooj that it was okay to laugh and that I was funny and that he should want to save me, but then the front door of the Mickeypot Tavern opened. We all looked towards the rectangle of natural light. And there, there was Gwen.

She was prettier than I'd remembered, even though it'd only been a week since I'd seen her last and nothing about her had changed. Maybe it was just that the lighting was worse. As she walked over, the old comedian, still hacking his guts up, plastered his swaying hairs to his head with one of his slimy hands.

"Shane, can I talk to you?" she said.

Her face was hardened into a mask of businesslike indifference, but it was the kind of indifference that didn't have much patience and wouldn't be indifferent for long. I stepped off my stool and it was like jumping into a rowboat with both feet the way the floor pitched beneath me. I tried to walk a straight line as I followed her over to a small table that was just far enough away from everyone to give us absolutely no privacy. As I sat down I tragically realized that I'd left my half-empty third pitcher on the bar. I also realized that I really had to piss.

We sat looking at each other and I tried to keep my head from swimming away.

"Shane, in spite of everything, I want you to know that I'm

sorry for the way things had to end for you at Panopticon." She was speaking slowly, measuring her words to show how serious all this was.

"Yeah," I said.

"It's over between us," she said, and she paused to give this the weight that it was obviously lacking. "But I think it's important that we talk about a few things, or else it's all just been a waste of everyone's time."

It was the speech she'd been rehearsing since the night we'd first met. For her, this was the payoff to all those brutal, meaningless nights together. I decided to be the bigger person. I decided to let her have this closure, this satisfaction. I would let her lecture me and teach me and then never think about her again.

"You're a good person inside Shane, but you need to realize that what you do on the outside affects other people. We all have an impact, whether we like it or not."

"You mean like the weather?" I said.

"What?"

"Like when a swallow flaps its wings in Africa and then there's a tsunami in Japan and then a building falls down in Kansas? I think that's just a myth really," I said. I decided to be the smaller person after all. I knew that I would.

"Don't embarrass yourself. I'm being serious. I don't have to do this you know. I'm just trying to help you. You hurt me Shane. But more than that, you hurt yourself."

"Yeah," I said.

"You can be such a great person when you open yourself up, when you let people in. But until you start doing that on a regular basis you're not going to grow, personally or professionally."

"Sometimes you have to clear cut a forest so that other small plants can flourish."

"You know what? I don't have to take this. I've put up with enough of your sarcasm. Your cynicism is a poison I'm not going to drink anymore," she said with great dignity.

I started laughing.

"I don't know what about this situation is funny to you. The bottom line is you screwed up. You made mistakes, big mistakes, and you need to take responsibility for them."

"Yeah."

"Making fun of a retarded man at work? Jesus Shane. I put myself out for you. I talked to my friends in HR *on your behalf* and this is what you do? How do you think that reflects on me?"

"I think your reputation will survive."

"That's not the point," she said.

"What is the point?"

"You should have gone to Martha's funeral. That's the point."

"I knew it."

"And while we're being honest, what's with you falling asleep in my bathroom all the time? Do you have some kind of sick fetish or something?"

"Uh, what?"

"And what about all the salt? Why did you dump all that salt in my bed?"

"Dump salt in your bed? Do you have any idea how ridiculous that sounds?"

"I know how ridiculous it sounds, that's why I'm asking you to explain it. The last time you stayed at my apartment I found two saltshakers wrapped up in my sheets after you left. Explain *that*."

That's where they were. Fuck.

"This isn't about me, or your bathroom, or saltshakers. This is about you. You have an eating disorder," I said.

She stiffened in her chair, her spine springing straight up like she'd had a much too successful scoliosis operation. Her eyes wet instantly at the corners.

"Who told you that?" she said.

"You have an eating disorder?"

"I did in college. It's not something you ever really get over," and she bowed her head.

I was unmoved. Come on, who didn't have a fucking eating disorder in college? That's like saying you had a Bob Marley poster, or that you stuck your roommate's toothbrush up your ass one time and then laughed as you watched him use it for the rest of the semester. Big fucking deal.

We sat in a silence that I was very comfortable with.

"No," she said, looking up at me, fighting her wet eyes without even wiping them. She was using sheer will alone. "No. I won't let you do that to me. I beat my food problem and it made me stronger. I won't let you tear me down with that now."

God, she was so valiant.

"Yeah," I said.

"Remember when I said I hadn't figured you out?" Her eyes were wide now like she was a fucking maniac.

"No."

"Well I was lying!"

I didn't give two shits one way or the other. I really had to piss.

"Do you want to hear what I figured out about you?"

"Not really."

"Do you want to know what you are?"

"Definitely not."

"You're a coward. And you're weak and afraid and you're a fake, fake person. You're a *fucking* phony. You pretend to care about other people but you don't."

"I never pretended to care," I said.

"That's all you ever did was pretend. But really the only person you care about is yourself."

"That's not true. I don't care about anything."

"The whole time we were together, it was all just a lie. Like that crucifix around your neck. It's just one of your props, like being a good listener. You're probably not even Catholic."

"I'm afraid of vampires."

"It's all just *bullshit!* You play yourself off as this totally different person and it's just *bullshit!*" She accented her curses strangely, like she wasn't used to saying them and felt a little embarrassed and empowered by them.

I rose to my own defense.

"That's not true. That's like you thinking I'm a ninja because I wear black pajamas to bed. Or in the fucking Viet Cong. It's not my fault you get your outfits confused."

"That is the stupidest thing I've ever heard," she said.

"Well, you're the one who wanted to get into this big gubernatorial debate about everything. I didn't go find you, you came in here."

"Now you're just trying to change the subject. You're blaming me because you're afraid. That's why it had to end like this. You're afraid to have a real life so you're hiding in this dirty, disgusting bar."

I looked over at Sooj to let him know that I obviously disagreed and thought the Mickeypot Tavern was a lovely, lovely place. He was not amused.

"You were afraid of stability and success so you threw your job away, by insulting the memory of a dead woman and making fun of a retarded man for god's sake."

I again tried to mug for Sooj, for one of the old men even, but it wasn't working.

"And you were afraid of a committed, healthy relationship, so you threw that away too. All because of fear and cowardice. You had a real chance to be happy Shane—"

"There was never that chance," I said.

"And you know what? You *fucked* it up. And you have to live with that."

"Somehow I'll get by."

"And now you have nothing. I hope you're happy. I hope you're finally happy being unhappy. That's the only kind of happiness a coward like you can know."

"That's so ironic."

"*Fuck you!*" And she jerked herself out of her chair so she was standing over me, foaming at the mouth. "You *fucking bastard!* I come down here trying to help you, trying to salvage something, *anything*, and this is how you treat me? *Fuck* you!"

She was livid, her fists shaking at her sides. I was smiling faintly. It was all very emotional.

"So?" she said as I smiled up at her.

"So what?"

"So what do you have to say for yourself?"

"About what?"

"About this?" she said, and waved her arms around the bar, exasperated.

I thought about it for a minute.

"I'm just not sure what you're looking for," I said.

"I'm looking for the truth."

"The truth about what?"

"About this!" And she waved her arms around again, even more frantically than last time. "About you! About why you're like this! I want an explanation!"

"Um."

"You need to hear it as much as I do," she said, trying to calm herself.

"There is no explanation."

"There has to be!" she shouted, her voice echoing off the mildewed walls.

"Why?"

"Just tell me!"

"What? Do you want to hear that a dental hygienist has been murdered and I'm the prime suspect?"

"You're drunk," she said.

"Or that I had to jerk off into a plastic bag and hand it to a detective named Sergeant?"

"You're disgusting."

"What, we're connecting! Isn't this wonderful?"

"EXPLAIN!!!" she screamed in my face.

"I'm in love with my landlord's wife! Is that what you want to hear?"

"What?" she said.

"Shit."

"What did you just say?"

"Um."

The scream was primordial. I have never heard another human being make such a sound. Her jaw distended like she was a snake about to eat a small child and her whole body shook, her two fists out like she was a pilot trying to pull a 747 out of a nose-dive. Then she lunged at me. I leaned back in my chair and put my leg up to defend myself, to fend her off, and she grabbed it with both hands and tore into my shin like it was a fucking turkey drumstick. Feeling her teeth go through my jeans and break skin I screamed and kicked with my other leg, toppling backwards out of my chair and sprawling on the floor.

What happened next was my own primal instinct taking over. It was like in a movie when two vampires are about to fight, a good vampire and a bad vampire—although it is hard to truly be a good vampire—and the fangs come out and there's that crazed look in both their eyes and it comes down only to who will be more savage. I wasn't proud of myself, but this was innate, one of those animal impulses that has been in Man since the days he lived in caves and howled at the full moon like a beast. I had no more control over my actions than the lion does when the taste for blood is on him. There are some instincts society can temper, but never tame.

So I ran away. Fast, like my ancestors had always done before me. It was how we had survived. I faked left and then scurried around a table and through a door and into the men's room where I barricaded myself in a stall—christ the lock was flimsy, the dead bolt as thick as a stick of Juicy Fruit—and I pressed all my quivering weight up against the thin, thin metal door. Gwen was still screaming as she barreled into it like a fucking battering ram, again and again, flinging me into the toilet with every shoulder she threw. The entire frame of the stall shook as her roars echoed off the grimed walls, but the lock held. She pummeled the door with her fists, denting it like cannonballs and caving in the metal, but the door would not fall.

"Come out here you sissy! You *fucking* cheating sissy *bastard!*" she screamed, but the intervals between her charges were growing longer. She was slowing down. I was safe now and I knew it.

"Leave me alone you fucking cannibal!" I shouted. "You hurt me during sex!"

"Come out here!" she screamed.

"Martha died in vain!" I shouted, and I laughed as she left a fist print in the metal right by my head.

"Deadly force is authorized!" I shouted, and I knew that Sooj was right.

It was strange, but I never felt closer to her than when I was cowering behind that bathroom stall door, cringing as she beat it into scrap metal.

Exhausted, and with bruised, bloodied fists, she left without saying goodbye. And after a long time I was able to take the piss I so desperately needed to take. And after even longer, I unlocked the door. It dropped from one hinge as it swung open.

The scene outside was as it had always been. The two old men were still at the bar, and Sooj was behind it with his arms folded, pissed off. It is good to have things you can count on. The only sign of nonsense was the overturned chair that I had fallen out of so long ago. I righted it, pushed it under the table, and everything was tidy again.

"Women," I said as I walked up to my stool.

"You," Sooj said, putting both hands on the bar and leaning forward. "Don't ever come in here again."

"But I need you for my alibi. From last night. I was here, right?" I said.

"I never seen you before. Get out."

I looked at the old men, both drooling in their alcoholic dementia. I looked at Sooj, for the last time. I grabbed a saltshaker off the bar and ran.

Chapter 9

I had a long, lonely, freaked out wait until Tuesday, and there was nothing I could do about it.

I had lost Sooj forever. I knew that now. And all of the depressingly silent camaraderie of the Mickeypot Tavern was gone too. I was alone. And drinking Miller High Life in cans in your salty apartment by yourself sounds immeasurably more sad than drinking it flat from dirty pitchers in a filthy bar flanked by drunk ass old men and the pissed off Cleveland-born son of Lebanese immigrants. So I bought a case of it from the liquor store and that's what I did for most of Monday, and really it wasn't immeasurably more anything. It was all right.

And then I went for a ride on my bike.

As bad a shape as I was in my bike was fucking worse. It was in the final stages of full-blown Parkinson's. Everything shook and went the wrong way and there was nothing anyone could do to save it. The tires wobbled almost parallel to the street and the handlebars had nothing to do with the steering anymore. Sometimes they could make a suggestion but usually I just had to go straight. If I needed to turn I had to drag my feet and stop, then pick the bike up and point it in the right direction like a blind old mule. The high seat had lost all its mooring so it bounced and swiveled completely around, sometimes while I was on it. It was like sitting on the propeller of a retarded man-child's beanie. That was what my life had become.

I rode the piece of shit more out of spite than convenience. I refused to throw it away. I wanted to break its spirit first. I wanted to be there when it finally fell apart. When it realized it had lost all purpose and meant nothing to no one and finally died, I wanted to stand there and laugh as I pissed all over it. That's what I was hanging on for. And if the breakdown happened while I was going down a hill or coasting through traffic I would definitely die too, but it would be worth it, so great was my hatred for that bike. I was locked in a death struggle of pride and bitterness, a consuming battle of wills with an inanimate object. If there was any meaning in that, I did not know what it was.

But I still rode it. The chain was worn and would slip randomly and leave me helplessly pedaling like a fat man on an elliptical machine, and then just as randomly it would catch and the sudden resistance would lift me off the seat and drive the wire catch of my tiny helmet straight into my throat. I would wince and swallow and that would drive the wire in again and further, skewering my Adam's apple like a fucking shish kebab. I knew that a punctured Adam's apple would mean an emergency tracheotomy and one of those voice boxes that embittered smokers use on commercials to bitch about cigarettes after their larynxes have been removed, and I didn't want to be one of those people, so I'd swallow again out of fear, the wire jabbing me again and harder. I couldn't stop.

It was a stupid vicious cycle and I knew exactly what I had to do to end it: stop being such a cheap ass and buy a new bike and a new fucking helmet, one that wasn't made for an eight year old. But I did nothing, and I knew that I never would. And that pissed me off, which was good because it at least distracted me from how drunk and afraid I was. I was in a bad mess and my bike wasn't getting me anywhere I needed to go. Soon I would have a voice box and sound like I was channeling the robot voice of deaf Marlene as I rotted in my tiny jail cell. It wouldn't be ironic. It would just be very sad.

Some days there's a song stuck in your head and you catch yourself whistling or humming it at inappropriate times, like on a crowded bus right into some stranger's face, or when you're standing at a urinal. It's awkward, and it gets annoying after a while hearing that same song over and over again, but it's really not so bad. Other days there's a song playing everywhere you go, like a soundtrack that you can't do a goddamn thing about. Those are the days it is clear that there are other forces at work, forces which you do not understand and over which you have no power. Those are the days men propose to their girlfriends or commit suicide or subscribe to a magazine they know they will never read or don't get on a plane that crashes an hour later, depending on what song is playing. My song that day wasn't really a song. It was one steady, wet blow on a didgeridoo, that long wooden gourd-looking instrument that Australian aborigines used to play right before they cannibalized an entire village or cut someone's dick off in a voodoo ritual. It was pretty fucking ominous.

That's why I'd bought a case of High Life and drank can after can hardly breathing. That's why I'd left my apartment. That was the soundtrack I was spastically pedaling away from.

I picked up speed downhill on a long street that was lined with upscale restaurants and coffeeshops and specialty stores with hardly any merchandise, a trendy strip that was always crowded with annoying people who had interesting conversations over lattes and dressed their kids like little, cuter versions of themselves. It was like a high class version of Mardi Gras how they walked in and out of places and then into the street like they owned everything, which they probably did. They always gave me dirty looks when I almost ran over their children, even though there was nothing I could do because of fate and no steering. But I didn't get any dirty looks that night, because there was nobody around. That night the street and all its buildings were deserted.

And I knew then that I was the victim of some great conspiracy. Whoever was playing the didgeridoo took a breath.

I felt the headlights behind me before I saw them. When I looked over my shoulder, my helmet wire stabbing me in the throat, I saw the car. It was about thirty yards away and closing on me fast, swinging to either side of the road. I pedaled frantically, uselessly as the chain refused to catch. I stood on the pedals and jerked the handlebars but nothing was working. I was coasting fast down the street hugging the curb, completely out of control. Whoever was playing the didgeridoo was totally freaking out, raising the pitch into inhuman registers. It sounded like Mumm-Ra's theme song from *Thundercats*.

Then the car was beside me. It was bright orange with tinted windows. The tires were huge and the engine was gunning loud. "01" was painted across the door in black. It was the fucking General Lee from *The Dukes of Hazzard*.

The whole world was still for a moment as I stood on my bike pedals and saw my reflection in the tinted window, saw my tiny helmet on top of my head, the car and I coasting down the street side by side. Then the world spun again, faster to catch up for the moment it had missed, and the General Lee swung to the far side of the street and then came tearing back at me.

What came next I will never understand.

I jumped, or I fell, from my bike right into a street sign pole, which miraculously snapped under my left armpit like we were both made of Lego. I hugged the pole and spun and spun full out like I was flying as the General Lee trampled my bike beneath its huge tires. Even as it was happening, I was singularly conscious of it being the coolest thing I had ever done in my life.

And then I stopped spinning and slid down the pole and I landed on my shoulder and hit my head and just missed breaking my face. And as I lay on the sidewalk the General Lee tooted its horn, playing a whining, dying Dixie. Then it sped off swerving down the street.

I spent the next day holed up in my salty apartment watching soap operas and writing out plans for my escape, which I immediately burned on my stove so the judge wouldn't see me as a flight risk when he was setting my bail. The ashes of my failed, untested plans blew all over my apartment and dirtied my pretty, pretty salt.

I had left my bike mangled on the side of the road the night before without even urinating on it, and I ran home in a crouch trying to stay low, hugging my right arm because my shoulder was throbbing. I ran awkwardly, but fast. I hid behind mailboxes and telephone poles when I could. Sometimes I jaywalked. My bike helmet had twisted around backwards but I kept wearing it anyway. It had saved me from a smashed head once already that night. I hoped it wouldn't have to again. People looked at me as I bolted past them, bent over and crying, and they kept looking as I shambled down the street. But the General Lee did not make another pass.

The adrenaline of cheating death and being cool had mostly worn off by the time I got home, but it completely fucking evaporated when I saw the blood on my neck. The wire catch in my helmet had left a gash from my Adam's apple to the tip of my spine. My fucking brain stem could have been compromised. I looked like I owed the Russian mob money. Another few inches either way and deep and I would have been decapitated. My shoulder was already yellow from where I'd landed on it. It was probably dislocated.

But the real kick in the ass was that it could have been anyone driving that car. Never in my life had so many people had so many seemingly legitimate reasons to kill me. Marlene's husband, Gwen, those detectives, maybe even Sooj. And that was just the people I knew. There were always other random lunatics or kids needing to murder someone before they could join a gang. But where would any of them get a *Dukes of Hazzard* General Lee replica? That was the greatest question of all. It was completely identical except for the tinted windows and the fact that it had door handles. It was the perfect novelty killing machine.

I immediately suspected Marlene's husband, but were deaf people even allowed to drive? They couldn't hear car horns or traffic updates on the radio. There was no way those fuckers at the DMV would give them licenses. It couldn't have been him.

And would Gwen really have cashed in her 401(k) just to buy a new car to run me down in? That wasn't her style. She'd rather tear me apart with her bare hands. And why the fuck would Sooj want to kill me anyway? Over a saltshaker?

I couldn't go to the police. They might've been the ones behind the whole thing. They had access to the repossessed vehicles lot. Maybe some moonshine-soaked hillbilly had blown his paycheck trying to be like Bo and Luke Duke and then had the car taken from him when he couldn't make his payments. I'd be much easier to convict posthumously. I'd be an even better scapegoat dead. The publicity and their promotions were worth more to them than my life. It's a shame when society has degenerated to the point where that's a legitimate possibility.

No, I was on my own. And this was bigger than whoever was driving that car. Bigger than the General Lee. First Marlene gets murdered, then somebody tries to kill me. But why? Why? What was the conspiracy? Was it about drugs? Women? Power? Revenge? What tied me to Marlene?

Doug. It was Doug. He was behind the assassinations. He'd freaked out when Marlene broke up with him and he killed her, and now he was trying to kill me for some reason. And he was going to frame some hillbilly for it. He was a criminal mastermind. But how could I prove it? The semen sample the cops found on Marlene. If it was in her ass, then Doug was her killer.

I needed to find out where that semen was lodged. Do they print that kind of thing in the obituaries? Could I go to the coroner and slip him a twenty? Would he think I was a perv? Would the detectives tell me? How do you even bring something like that up?

You don't. Whatever the circumstances, no matter what's at

stake, you just don't. I can't usually think of anything worth dying for, but I can say to this day that I'd rather get murdered than have to ask somebody if there's semen in a deceased deaf woman's ass.

And Doug was no criminal mastermind. Men with strawberry blond hair aren't capable of that kind of calculation. Fuck, I didn't know what was going on.

I'd have to do some research. Start with the details, start with what I knew, and then the whole thing would come into focus on its own. It was like those stupid jigsaw puzzles that I was never any good at, except this time I didn't even have the picture on the front of the box to guide me. Okay, first I had to find out who'd just tried to kill me. That was fairly urgent. Once I knew that, it would lead me to Marlene's killer, if they weren't the same person. And then, all would be revealed.

So, I needed to check the papers for car listings, see where somebody could rent or buy a General Lee. That's where I'd begin. Then I would conduct surveillance. I would use the Internet somehow. I used to watch *Magnum, P.I.* every day after school—it came on right after *The Facts of Life*—and I'd read a few *Encyclopedia Brown* mysteries and done book reports on them too. I knew how to solve things. And I would. Right after I talked to Bryce's wife.

The only weapon I had in my apartment was a dull knife, but I took it with me when I went to see her the next day. I was an hour early but I didn't care. I had to talk to someone, and I could trust her. At least I thought I could. If I couldn't, that's what the knife was for. It was a butter knife, the kind that's on the tiny plate at fancy restaurants, the one that looks like the puffed out sail of a small boat. They were very good for spreading. If it got ugly I'd pull it on her. Then I could slink away in shame as she was doubled over laughing at me.

I took the stairs, and when I came out on her floor my stomach fell into my ass. Bryce and Mobo were at the end of the hallway. They were standing in front of Bryce's door, huddled together, conspiring. It was a conspiracy. I was too far away to hear anything, but Mobo was doing all the talking. Bryce was just nodding mutely. He looked sad. Then Mobo reached into his black leather trenchcoat and took out a small package wrapped in brown paper and handed it to Bryce, and Bryce shoved an envelope towards him that Mobo slipped into his coat with one fluid, practiced motion. He started talking again but Bryce jerked his head up and saw me standing dumb and fascinated at the end of the hall. He said something quick to Mobo, and Mobo looked over at me and smiled. Bryce ducked out the side door clutching the package to his stomach as Mobo walked down the hall towards me with his arms out, his trenchcoat flowing behind him.

"Shane!" He dragged my name out, sounding happy to see me. "My cholo. What's the word?"

"Hey Mobo," I said, gripping the butter knife behind my back.

"What do you say champa?"

"You late on your rent again?" And I nodded towards the door that had just closed behind Bryce.

"Always my man, always," he said, and laughed. "You never came back up to see me." But he said it playfully, like I hadn't offended him at all.

"Yeah, I've been pretty busy."

"I've heard." And he looked at me like he knew something. I didn't like it. "Listen," he said, and leaned in close like he'd been doing with Bryce. My arm tensed but I didn't stab or spread him. "The way things are going around here you might want to come talk to me soon."

"Why's that?"

"Opportunity monchuro, opportunity. Everything's a business, whether we like it or not. And everybody's either a partner, or a competitor. We all got to choose sides sometimes chamumbo."

"Is that what you and Bryce were doing? Choosing sides?"

He smiled.

"Attorney-client privilege my friend. We all have to pick our horses, you know what I'm saying?"

I didn't have a goddamn clue.

"Yeah, you know how it is," he said, and smiled at me. "Things are changing chamanga. They're changing fast. I just want to make sure a chupo like you doesn't end up on the outside."

"Thanks," I said, wondering who the fuck this guy was and what he was offering.

"There's money out there to be made cobrana, there's things to be had if you want them bad enough. We're still playing by the law of the west out here, every day. That cowboy shit never dies. Every day pucho, every day."

"Yeah," I said, thinking about it. "Maybe I'll stop by later on and see what you've got for me."

He clapped his hands.

"Now you're in the game gambilo. To las minas muertes,

that's how it has to be!" And he pointed at me with his fingers on either side of his head like he was a bull about to charge, or like he was giving me the evil eye, or like he was a fucking imbecile. "I'll see you soon," he said, then moved past me into the stairwell, his leather coat flowing behind him.

Things had to be bad if I was considering taking this dipshit seriously. But things, things were bad.

I waited until he had gone up the stairs before I walked down the hall and knocked, because no matter what else is going on in your life adultery should always be discreet. She opened the door in her robe and narrowed her eyes at me, annoyed, and I remembered that I was an hour early. But she still went into the bedroom, and I followed. And after some halting, tentative, terrible sex that didn't last very long at all we laid on her bed and she smoked a cigarette. I did not. I would have refused even if she'd offered me one. I felt more like a guppy than the majestic, sexual tuna I thought I had become.

She was smoking just to get it over with, sucking in long and then blowing right out like she was gulping down a drink she didn't want. I was ashamed. I showed up early and finished early and I'd be told to leave before my time had even really begun. I had nowhere else to go.

"I hurt my shoulder," I said, hoping it would somehow explain everything.

The tip of her cigarette glowed orange in the dark. I waited.

"All right, I don't want to freak you out," I said, and took a breath, "but someone is trying to kill me."

"Is it Bryce?"

Jesus fucking christ. I hadn't thought of that.

"I didn't, think so." *Shit.* "Why, is he?"

"Is he what?" she said.

"Is he trying to kill me?" I was working very, very hard to keep my voice under control. I wanted to scream like a little girl on the playground whose pigtails were being pulled by a mean boy.

"I wouldn't worry about Bryce," she said.

"I wasn't." *Until fucking now.*

"He would never intentionally hurt someone."

"How about unintentionally?"

"Maybe, but anybody can do that. You can't really predict those kind of things."

"What about Mobo?" I said.

She opened her lips on her cigarette, then finished the smaller drag she was taking.

"What about him?" She blew smoke up towards the fan.

"What's his story?"

"He has a pet guinea pig."

That he fucks until it shrieks for mercy. I wondered if she knew about that.

"That's it?" I said.

"He wears a black leather trenchcoat. He looks like a pharaoh."

He certainly did. That much was fucking true. She smoked her cigarette down and crushed it out and then lit another. I knew she wasn't telling me everything.

"So what do you think?" I said.

"About what?"

"About the situation?"

"What do you mean?"

"I mean me? Getting murdered?" My voice was an octave too high but there was nothing I could do about it.

She looked at me.

"You'll be fine," she said.

"What about Bryce and Mobo?"

"They'll be fine too."

"But could they be in on it?"

She blew out smoke and lowered her eyebrows like she hadn't been following the conversation.

"In on what?"

"On my assassination?" I was ready to fall apart.

"You think it's some kind of conspiracy?" she said, smiling.

"Maybe." I was shattering into tiny pieces.

Then she laughed.

"If there is a conspiracy to have you killed I doubt Bryce or *Mobo* are part of it," she said. And even though she was mocking me it was comforting to hear.

"Not an important part anyway," she added.

And that was less comforting.

I watched the smoke twist under the ceiling fan and I thought about crying, literally fucking breaking down and curling up on her shoulder so she could rock me and whisper to me and quiet me until I fell asleep. But I couldn't. I don't think she could either. Maybe she could have, but you never know with those sort of things. Unless you're in rehab or married to a nice lady or paying a complete stranger for it you usually can't. It's flawed and it's a shame but that's how it works.

"Could you tell Bryce to go bowling on Thursday nights too?" I said, which maybe was my way of doing the same thing.

"I can't," she said.

We lay there for a long time and I was thinking. She was smoking slower and making it last and I thought about my fortune cookie: "The world is your oyster, but you are allergic to shellfish." It would be a good fortune cookie. Maybe it would be important to someone at just the right time. People put their faith in strange things and give credence to all kinds of unintentional signs and symbols and stars, so why not a slip of paper inside a lump of Chinese dough? It was your fortune after all.

It would be a good fortune cookie, but it would be a better bumper sticker, slapped on the back of an eighteen-wheeler and driven all over the country for people and tourists to see. And in that inevitable twelve-car pileup after the tractor trailer had jackknifed, those same people and tourists would inch by in their cars, staring out their windows, and they'd see "The world is your oyster, but you are allergic to shellfish" on the detached bumper of that totaled wreck, slowly being engulfed by flames. And maybe they would finally understand.

"I thought of a good bumper sticker," I said.

"Do you even own a car?"

"No," I said.

And all the world seemed hopeless and against me.

Chapter 10

There wasn't much left to do after that. I made some vague, half-assed plans to tail Bryce and Mobo, maybe even Doug. I wanted to see him get his head smashed in a bus door once before I died, and apparently I didn't have much time left.

But I didn't tail anyone. What was I going to do, run around after them like fucking Mr. Bean, hiding behind bushes and pretending I was a statue whenever they turned around? I didn't have a car. I didn't even have my shitty bike anymore. The best I could do was an old pair of binoculars and a cheap Spy-Tech listening microphone that I'd picked up at Goodwill. It had a range of four feet and no batteries. I was fucked.

So I sat in my apartment wallowing in salt and I waited for the other shoe to drop and kick me in the face. Sometimes I went out and walked slowly past the Mickeypot Tavern on the far side of the street, casting furtive, girlish glances at the door. But no one ever came out looking for me. No one came out to welcome me back home. Sooj did not care.

I was hoping some terminal illness euphoria would kick in,

and that since I knew I had a death sentence hanging over me I'd immediately learn to cherish each day and every breath as a beautiful, wondrous gift from the God I now desperately believed in, and that I'd vow not to waste any more of my precious life that would very soon be ending. Then I could go out and hug strangers and sing out loud and twirl around on top of a mountain like the fucking *Sound of Music* and be inspirational and brave. Maybe then I could finally do all the things I'd been putting off all these years.

Unfortunately I didn't know what any of them were. It takes more than one kick in the pants to reverse a lifetime of unplanned apathy. I should have been keeping track all along like Gwen. Then I could have just gone down the list. But even that wouldn't have helped. It takes a special, ironic kind of person to use their own impending death as an impetus to finally live. Maybe I could use someone else's death for that, but my own only scared the shit out of me and made me want to hide. And having a terminal illness is different than probably getting mowed down by the General Lee the next time you step out your front door. There's nothing brave about getting hit by a car.

I thought a little bit about Bryce's wife, and how she'd never asked me why I thought someone was trying to kill me. That bothered me some, but not in the suspicious way that it should have. It just bothered me.

The only thing that helped me forget that I was fucked, for a little while at least, was a bubble bath. I hadn't taken one in years. It was surprisingly frothy. And sitting in that small tub with my bare knees bent up in the air, soaking in my own filth, I felt so good and ridiculous it was almost right. As I began to prune and shrivel I thought about going to the police and falsely confessing

to everything, anything they wanted, just to get it over with. After a few years a college journalism class would review my trial
and see that I was obviously innocent. There would be embarrassing publicity. The governor would grant me a pardon and I'd
be released. At my press conference I'd say, "I knew God would
make this day happen. In my heart, I was always free." And then
I would weep. And then I would sue the shit out of the city and
the mayor's office and the police department and anybody else I
could find, to make sure that no one would ever have to suffer
such terrible freedom in their heart again.

I would be rich, and I would have my redemption. It was very
Christ-like in the end. I'd just have to put up with all those brutal ass rapings every day for a few years, and try not to get
shanked during any riots. That was not very Christ-like. But it's
the question all of us have to answer at some point: how much is
your ass worth to you?

I would not go to the police. And fuck those sanctimonious
college kids too.

I went to the movies instead. If I had to die it would be as I
had always lived: like Abraham Lincoln. I had a twelve-second
complete nervous breakdown as I walked into the theater and
saw how huge and open it was. Stadium seating has made it
much easier to be assassinated at the movies. After a frantic de-
liberation I sat in the back row in the corner, so no one could
sneak up on me. There were no emergency exits nearby and it
would be harder to escape, but I figured if I saw anyone coming
for me I'd yell, "He's got a gun!" and then get lost in the fleeing
mass hysteria. There would at least be other bodies to stop some
of the bullets.

As I sat there imagining this attempt on my life two high

school kids sat beside me and surprised me and I almost went into shock. They started feeling each other up immediately, before the previews even started, even though I was right beside them freaking out. They looked like they were both eleven years old. They were small, but would make good human shields.

The movie was a remake of *The Maltese Falcon*, set in modern-day Los Angeles. Critics had said it was "gritty" and "edgy" and "astonishing." The Humphrey Bogart role was played by an actor who'd gotten his start on *The Mickey Mouse Club* a few years before. That's where he'd learned his craft. He looked about the same age as the high school kid getting the handjob beside me. The guy playing Peter Lorre's part had been in Menudo. His solo debut a year earlier had been a crossover sensation, and his newest single, "Ha Cha Cha!" was available exclusively on *The Maltese Falcon* soundtrack.

I recognized the Fat Man from soup commercials, and the women all seemed to be playing the same role, which I didn't remember even being in the original. They spent most of the movie taking showers and firing automatic weapons. At the end everyone had a dance off to see who would keep the falcon. Even the soup guy was shaking his ass to "Ha Cha Cha!"

In the middle of the dance off one of the women, who was straddling a folding chair like a stripper—all of the women danced like strippers actually—stood up suddenly and flung the chair away from her to show how empowered she was by her partial nudity. It flew across the room and knocked the Maltese Falcon off the table. She had been sexy yet inexplicably clumsy throughout the entire movie, and I finally understood why. As the falcon shattered on the floor in slow motion everyone gasped, with quick-cut close ups on each of their shocked and horrified yet slyly comedic faces. Then they realized it had been a fake all along. The real falcon was still at that evil pimp's house, being guarded by a team of deadly knife-wielding bitches. But that didn't matter. They all looked at each other and laughed, then started dancing again. The End.

If disgust was a shotgun I would've blown my own head off.

I waited until the credits were finished before I left. I always do, whether I'm about to be murdered or not. Sometimes there's an extra scene or some throwaway lines or outtakes that nobody else sees because they're already gone. There usually isn't, and even if there is it's never any good, but at least everyone else missed it. That's the most satisfying part of any movie for me.

The Maltese Falcon did have an extra scene. It was a digital mock-up of Humphrey Bogart and Peter Lorre, their real heads transposed onto the bodies of other actors. They were having their own dance off, while the rest of the new cast stood around clapping and shouting. Then Bogart and Lorre faced each other and did the Kid 'n Play dance from *House Party*, both of them standing on one foot and touching their free feet together in midair as they spun and flapped their arms while the cast chanted, "Go Humphrey, it's your birthday! Go! Go! Go Humphrey!" Then the lights came on.

I had to step over the high school kids on my way out. They were still going at it. They were in love.

I was too consumed by loathing to fear for my own life anymore. How were people supposed to solve crimes these days with such shitty movies for mentors? I went in there looking for some old-fashioned Bogart advice, some ideas about how to be a real detective or at least how to act when everyone thinks you're a murderer. Instead I got Mickey Mouse matching wits with

Menudo. I got an old man who held a can of soup up next to his head and said, "Mmm mmm good" in the middle of the god-damn movie for no other reason than a campy laugh and a tie-in promotion. Who fires an AK-47 in the shower? Wouldn't you go deaf? It was all gone to shit. If only I had danced more, none of this would have ever happened.

I was actually enjoying my hatred for a while. It was righteous and good. Until I realized that I was very, very lost. Luckily my innate sense of navigation and survival had led me down a poorly lit street that was completely deserted.

Shit.

"TURN AROUND!" a pinched, atonal voice shouted be-hind me, and I immediately knew that it was going to end badly.

"DO YOU KNOW WHO I AM?"

I recognized him from the night he'd almost knocked me off the steps at Marlene's party. I recognized his nearly incompre-hensible voice from that time on the phone when I'd been tough. And it wasn't like I fucking knew that many deaf guys.

Marlene's husband. His eyes were close together and drilled deep into his skull, and his broad lunatic forehead glowed or-ange under the dim streetlight. He was standing with his legs apart, just far enough away so that he couldn't reach out and strangle me. His arms were at his sides and he kept clenching and unclenching his fists.

"YOU'RE GOING TO PAY FOR WHAT YOU DID!" he shouted.

The street was empty except for a plastic bag that skipped between us like a tumbleweed in the bullshit western that my life had become.

"YOU KILLED MY WIFE!"

No I didn't. I swear! I signed, shocked that I still remembered sign language. It was a much less impressive example of that phenomenon where a ninety-eight-pound mother can lift a Buick over her head with one hand if her baby is trapped underneath. *I'm sorry about Marlene, but I didn't do anything to her. She was my friend.*

He seemed as surprised as I was that I knew sign language.

You're a liar! he signed. *I know what you did to her. I found her in the bathroom.*

Listen, whatever happened to her, I had nothing to do with it. I already talked to the police and—

"THE POLICE DON'T CARE!" he shouted.

"You think just because I drew that picture of her we were having an affair?" I said, exaggerating my words so he could read my lips. "That's ridiculous."

What are you talking about? What picture?

Fuck.

Then it hit him.

The one of her sitting on garbage? he signed, getting noticeably more furious. "THE ONE IN OUR FUCKING BEDROOM!"

Fuck.

He took a step closer and I took a step back and put my hands up, palms out, like you're supposed to do when you're about to be attacked by a bear.

"I swear, we were just friends," I said.

"SWEAR ON YOUR LIFE!"

"I swear on my life," I said, even though I didn't feel comfortable doing it.

"YOU'RE LYING TO ME! YOU'RE LYING TO MY FACE JUST LIKE YOU LIED ON THE PHONE! JUST LIKE YOU LIED TO THE POLICE!"

I had to listen hard to understand him. He kind of sounded like a whale song, but I pretty much got what he was saying.

"No I didn't," I said.

"I FOLLOWED YOU!"

"What?"

"FROM THE BOWLING ALLEY TO YOUR APARTMENT! ALL THOSE NIGHTS, I FOLLOWED YOU!"

"Bowling alley?" I said. Oh jesus.

"I FOLLOWED THE TWO OF YOU BACK THERE. I KNOW WHAT YOU DID."

"No, that was my landlord!" I said, excited. "He goes bowling all the time. I'll show you where he lives."

"DO YOU THINK I'M STUPID! I KNOW WHAT I SAW!"

"Did you really see my face? Look at my face." And I tilted my head up to the orange streetlight. "Me and him are the same height, that's probably why you thought—you didn't see my face, did you."

He hesitated for a second, and that's when I should have run. But I was much too satisfied with what a fantastic detective I'd become, and with what all this new information could mean for me. I kind of felt like dancing.

I know it was you, he signed, cold and ominously calm. He reached into his pocket and I took another step back and was afraid, but he pulled out a folded piece of paper instead. When he unfolded it I was afraid again.

"EXPLAIN THIS!" he shouted, waving it at me. It was the $800 check Marlene had made out to me. I saw Marvin the Martian with his hands on his hips in the upper right-hand corner.

Shit.

"YOU CAN'T EXPLAIN? I'LL DO IT FOR YOU. YOU

HAD AN AFFAIR WITH MY WIFE, AND THEN YOU
TRIED TO BLACKMAIL HER. SHE PAID AS MUCH AS
SHE COULD, AND WHEN THAT WASN'T ENOUGH
YOU KILLED HER. YOU FUCKED MY WIFE AND THEN
YOU KILLED HER FOR A FEW HUNDRED DOLLARS!"
he shouted atonally, shaking the check at me. Then he dropped
his head, sobbing.

I had to admit, it was a pretty good story. I would have
thought the same thing if I was him. And there was no way I
could explain the truth without pissing him off even more. He
wouldn't have believed me anyway. No one likes to doubt their
own detective work, especially when their dead wife is involved.

No, I would be running away, and screaming like a woman as
I went. There had to be someone around who would help me.
And he was deaf so that probably meant he was slow, though I
was not sure why. I just had one last thing I needed to know.

"Where did you get the car from?" I said.

"WHAT?"

The car, I signed. "The General Lee," I said.

What are you talking about?

"The *Dukes of Hazzard* car, where did you get it from? Were
the doors welded shut?"

"YOU THINK THIS IS FUNNY?" he raged incomprehen-
sibly. "YOU THINK THIS IS ALL A JOKE?"

He reached into his jacket again.

"HOW ABOUT NOW? WHY AREN'T YOU LAUGHING
NOW?"

I wasn't laughing because he was pointing a gun at me. I'd
never seen a real gun before. Not in person. Not up close. I
never knew how big the barrel looked when it was pointed at

you. I couldn't stop staring at it. It was gravitational. It was fucking huge.

"Just wait," I said, stepping back and putting my hands up.

"YOU KILLED MARLENE!" he shouted, his whole hand rolling at the wrist, the gun shaking. "YOU FUCKED MY WIFE!"

"No," I said.

"YOU KILLED HER FOR MONEY!" He was blinking the tears out of his eyes as he shook the check at me.

"No. Please. Wait."

"YOU FUCKED MARLENE!" Tears were streaming down his face. Then his finger twitched and he pulled the trigger.

I was in a car accident back in high school, two days after I got my license. I was making a left turn at a light at the top of a hill and I was gunning it because the light had just turned yellow. But there was another car trying to beat the light from the other direction, coming up the hill from the other side, and he was flying. Just as I crossed lanes to turn I saw him, and in the split second before he hit me I yelled, "FUCK!" But it happened so fast all I could get out was "FU" before he slammed into the front of my car and spun me around the intersection like the asphalt was a sheet of ice. I kept yelling "FUUUUUU" as my car pirouetted and then got broadsided by another car. I was in a coma for two days and I swear all I heard was "FUUUUUU" the whole time I was out. That's the sound I woke up to.

And that was the sound I heard when he squeezed the trigger. That was all. My life didn't flash before my eyes, there were no epiphanies or revelations or beautiful memories. Just "FUU-UUUU."

There was a flash as the gun went off and I closed my eyes.

When I opened them he was staring at me, his eyes wide, and his hand was in ribbons. Blood fell to the sidewalk in spurts. The backfiring gun was a mess of blown-out metal, blackened and smeared red. He dropped it to the sidewalk and watched it fall. He looked at me again. And then he wailed. Holding his blood-soaked wrist, bent over, he wailed like a deaf man in agony. It sounded like a live cow being fed ass-backwards into a meat grinder. Then he fell to the ground.

I heard a siren far off, finally.

I reached down and picked up the $800 check just before the widening pool of blood caught it. And then I ran.

I got what I needed from my apartment and then I got out. I took a room at a cheap motel downtown. It was filthy. There were cigarette burns everywhere and piss stains on the mattress. The whole room smelled like rubber bands and old people. It was like being back at the Mickeypot Tavern except this place had a bathtub. A bathtub with dried blood smeared all along its rim. The toilet made me sad and in the bathroom mirror, with a bare lightbulb swinging just over my head, I looked like I had jaundice.

So I left and stayed at a Best Western instead. It was very elegant. I watched a lot of TV. And on Tuesday I went to see Bryce's wife.

She seemed surprised to see me when she opened the door. I liked it.

"A lot of people are looking for you," she said.

"I know," I said, looking right into her blue eyes and holding them, until she turned and walked towards the bedroom, untying her robe as she crossed the floor.

Our canned tuna sex was transcendent. The edges were still jagged and razor sharp where we'd been pried open, but inside it was wet and salty, tender, and softly breaking to pieces. We used the whole bed and went slow. We held on to each other and closed our eyes. We were one fish, moving in rhythm through cool water. It was good. No matter who you are or what you try to tell yourself, everyone has to eat sometimes. The off duty clown took out a loaf of bread and some lettuce, and he was happy with the sandwich he had made.

We lay back with our cigarettes and I tried to blow a huge smoke ring that would hover over us like a halo. Instead I coughed out clouds that curled towards the ceiling fan and scattered.

I finished my cigarette and got out of bed. I couldn't tell for sure but I think she was surprised again. I was finally unpredictable.

"Listen," I said as I started to get dressed, "it's been a strange couple of months around here. I know that. And a lot of things haven't made sense to me until now."

"Shane wait," she said, using my name, and she didn't sound disinterested like usual. She sounded flushed, maybe a little worried, and it just about killed me. I wanted to dive back into bed and stop pretending I was cool and pull her close to me and fall asleep. But instead I held up my hand, my two fingers and my thumb out like Jesus saying "Peace be with you." She sucked on her cigarette and let me continue. I was unpredictable and Christ-like, all in the same night.

"I know some people have been looking for me, and they probably told you some things. Maybe some bad things. But that doesn't matter. Whoever they were, whatever they said, it's not important. I can't explain it to you right now, but I will."

She opened her mouth to interrupt me but I kept talking. I needed to make this speech. I hadn't thought of anything else all week at the Best Western.

"We still have some things to decide, you and me. But right now the only thing that matters is what we do next. Then we'll see what comes out of it, either way."

I was watching her as I spoke, trying to read in her face if I was giving the right speech or not. I couldn't really tell, but I thought that I was.

"I have to take care of something tonight, and then it will be done. By tomorrow morning, everything should be a lot easier. For both of us," I said.

I turned to go.

"Wait," she said, sitting up, the bedsheet falling around her. "Don't do anything—"

"Stupid? Don't worry."

"No," she said, "not stupid. Just don't do anything."

There was something plaintive in her voice, a faint note of pleading that made my chest ache as I heard it, although I wasn't quite sure what it was for. Maybe she meant that some things have their own momentum and you shouldn't fuck around with them. You're not supposed to. They're not yours. Maybe she meant something else. Maybe she just wanted me to stay. Maybe she knew what would happen next.

"Trust me," I said. I'd never said that to anyone before. It made me feel like a hero. And I looked at her heroically, my shoulders back, my jaw set, pretending I was being photographed for a movie poster. Then I went outside to wait for her husband.

I stood behind the Dumpsters and prayed that I wouldn't see any rats or wolverines, anything that could jump out of the trash and maul or frighten me. I couldn't be in hysterics when Bryce showed up. I needed to be calm, in control. I needed to be cool. It seemed like hours and probably was, but then I saw him coming up the walkway. His head was down and his hands were in his pockets. He scuffed his boots as he walked, scraping his soles on the concrete.

I waited until he was at the door, until he'd put the key in, before I came up behind him. "Bryce!" I said, louder than I'd wanted to, so loud that it kind of scared me. But it scared him too. That was good. That was how I wanted it to be.

"Oh, Shane. Hi. You, scared me," he said, and laughed like he wasn't sure if it was a joke.

"Listen Bryce," I said, looking over my shoulder, "we don't have much time. I think you know why I'm here."

"No, uh, no. What do you mean?" he said and started scratching the back of his neck, his eyes shifting back and forth like a panicked villain.

"We don't have time for this," I said, trying to sound stern, but I was shrill instead. I coughed and cleared my throat. "I'm coming to you as a friend Bryce. You know what this is about."

"No, sorry. Uhm, I've got to go now. Big day tomorrow," he said, and turned to the door.

"I know about Tuesday nights Bryce," I said low, into the

back of his head. "I know what you've been doing. And so do the police."

When he turned around the look on his face may have been worth it. He was like a dead fish the way his mouth was wide open, but his eyes were fucking jumping out of his head like he was being strangled. I kept my face blank, just like his wife had taught me.

I wasn't exactly sure what I was talking about, but I had a few theories. And instead of going through all the trouble of trying to prove them I figured I'd just throw something at him and see what happened. He was already so high-strung even the vaguest accusation, even if it was only close to being true, would have been enough to send him jumping out a window. He just couldn't call my bluff, which is what these things always come down to in the end.

"Who told you?" he said. He was terrified. I was the greatest detective ever.

"That's not important."

"It's important to me!"

"Bryce, there's no time."

"But I had nothing to do with it!"

"You think that matters? You think that matters to the police?" I said. "All they care about is what they think they can prove. They work everything else around to make it fit."

"Oh god, I can't go to jail. I can't! It wasn't my idea. I told them, I wasn't even a part of it really! What am I supposed to do?"

"Bryce, I shouldn't even be here. I'm putting myself at risk just by—"

"Please! What do I do?" His voice was breaking.

"You know what you have to do. Just don't tell anybody about it. Not even your wife. And forget we had this conversation."

"Oh god. Oh god," he kept saying, tearing chunks out of the back of his neck with his fingernails. It was fucking gross.

"All right," I said, disgusted. "I've got to go."

"Okay." He was staring at the ground, clawing at his neck as I walked away.

"Shane!" he yelped after me, right before I turned the corner.

"Yeah?"

"Thanks," he said. "For everything."

I nodded.

Then I went up to my apartment and paced around and waited. He'd probably killed Marlene, I'd figured out that much. It was either him or Doug, after she broke it off with them, and Doug was too tragically humiliating and weird to kill anybody. Bryce was nervous enough to be capable of murder. You just can't trust high-strung people in certain situations. Like messy breakups, or Vietnam.

So it was probably Bryce. It had to be. And I was giving him a pass. He'd killed Marlene and I was letting him get away with it. That was a shame. But with him gone things would be much simpler. There'd be fewer questions, less mess. The police would find him eventually, or Marlene's one-handed husband would track him down and beat him to death with his prosthetic fist. It would be better that way. Vigilante justice is more satisfying, for everyone involved.

Either way he'd be gone in half an hour. Maybe less. He'd throw some clothes in a bag and take off. She probably wouldn't even ask him where he was going. She didn't care. But should I go to her tonight or wait until morning? I didn't want to seem eager. I'd wait.

Then tomorrow I'd show up and there'd be no need to explain. It would all be taken care of. Then we'd take off ourselves, after we gave the police the story they wanted to hear, blaming Bryce for everything. Or maybe we'd stick around for a while. I could be a landlord. I would be ruthless, but fair.

She'd know what I'd done. She probably knew already. But she wouldn't know how exactly. She wouldn't know what I'd said to Bryce to give him that petrified look as he frantically stuffed his clothes into a garbage bag and ran out the door without saying goodbye. And I'd never tell her. There would always be that mystery between us. That mystery is important.

Then I heard it.

Then I heard it again.

If I'd learned anything in the past week it was what a gunshot sounded like, and I knew I'd just heard two. And I was pretty sure where they'd come from.

Then it was silence.

I stood in the middle of my apartment rooted to the floor in mid-stride, stricken, sure I'd shatter if I tried to move. I managed to fall over like a pile of blocks all at once onto my bed, and I lay there listening. There was silence, still, and I pulled the sheet up over my head. Just over my head, draping it over my face like a shroud.

And that's where I hid. I hid there until I heard the sirens, and for a long time after that. Cowardice, when done correctly, can be its own kind of bravery.

Chapter 11

"Where have you been all week?" Detective Sikes said the next day. We were standing on the sidewalk outside my building. The sun was out. It was a nice day. To look at it you wouldn't have thought there'd been a shooting the night before. There was no crime scene, no yellow tape blocking any doorways. No city blocks were roped off. I didn't hear any sirens. Murder isn't such a big deal after all.

"Down at the Best Western," I said.

"Nice place?"

"Very elegant."

"You should have come in that night, after what happened with the husband," Sikes said. He wasn't cocky like before. There was nobody he had to impress. And he was much nicer now that he knew I hadn't killed anybody. "I can understand why you didn't, but you should have."

"Yeah," I said.

"Maybe it wouldn't have ended up like this."

"Thanks."

"Not that it was your fault really. Not all of it anyway," he said, and smiled. "Marlene Burton was having an affair. Guy lived in your building too."

"I know."

"Rick Beekman."

"I beg your pardon?"

"Rick Beekman. He was in the apartment right above you actually."

"You mean Mobo?"

"Yeah, that's what he kept telling us to call him. 'My name is not Rick Beekman. Rick Beekman is dead to me,' he kept saying."

"Mobo's real name is Rick Beekman?"

"Yep. But we came up with a few other names for him down at the station," he said.

So they'd shoved the old splintered baton up Mobo's ass and called him Sally. You hate to see that.

"And *he* was having the affair with Marlene?" I said.

"Yep. Pretty sick, huh?"

"Oops."

"What's that?"

"Uh, nothing." So I wasn't the greatest detective ever. Sometimes people make mistakes. The important thing is that you learn from them.

"We came by your place the next day to see if you were all right, but it looked like you'd taken off in a hurry. We figured you left town."

"How did you get into my apartment? The door was locked this time."

"You want to ask questions or you want me to tell you what happened?" he said, annoyed.

"I'm sorry. Please, go on."

"Okay," and he exhaled. "We went down to your landlord's place to see if maybe he knew where you were, and when he opened the door he was shaking. Then when we flashed our badges he fell apart. Most people get a little nervous, we're used to that, but this guy could barely stand."

"Was he scratching his neck?"

"I thought he was gonna pull his fucking head off. I was getting sick just looking at him. I almost cuffed him, just to make him stop," and he laughed. "But the way he was acting we knew he had to be up to something. And we didn't have anything else to do that day so we brought him in for questioning, gave him that whole 'You don't need a lawyer, don't make trouble for yourself' speech in the back of the car on the way in, same one we gave you. Sorry about that by the way."

"It's quite all right," I said.

"You have to admit, that's a good bit we've got there. You should've seen your face."

"I was fine. I'm very brave."

"You were better than this Bryce guy, I'll give you that. He just kept mumbling about how he had nothing to do with it and he didn't used to be like this, but we could barely understand him because he was crying so hard. We had to go easy on him. We were afraid he'd piss his pants. We had a guy do that once. Had to rip out all the upholstery in the backseat. Car still smelled like piss six months later."

"Yikes."

"We couldn't get much because of all the sobbing, but we did find out that he'd seen a deaf woman who fit Marlene Burton's description singing down at Kahuna Karaoke."

"Kahuna Karaoke?"

"That tiki bar on Grand, across the street from the bowling alley."

"I see."

"He used to go down there every Tuesday and Thursday night to sing. Said he used to be in a band."

"Funk," I said.

"That's what he told us. I didn't see it."

"Me neither."

"He said he didn't know who the girl was, but he'd seen her with Beekman before."

"Did Bryce call him Beekman too? How come everyone knew he wasn't Mobo except me?"

"You want me to finish the story?"

"Yes."

"Okay. So we go to Beekman's apartment and he opens the door with no shirt on and says, 'Who sent you?' real suspicious. 'Bryce,' I said. 'Your landlord.' Then he relaxes and invites us in. Told us to sit Indian style on his leopard-print rug while he waited for his press-on tattoo to dry. A dragon on his right arm. The guy was so skinny it wrapped all the way around on itself. Dragon's head was up its own ass," he said, and laughed. "Then he pulls out a briefcase and asks us how much we're looking for."

"Fireworks?"

"Drugs."

"Nice."

"Yeah, real nice. Turns out he's been dealing down at Kahuna Karoake, selling baggies to all the accountants and kindergarten teachers who like to cut loose and sing "Sweet Caroline" and "Dancing Queen" every night after work. They like to pretend they're real rock stars and blow lines in the bathroom with rolled-up dollar bills before they go onstage."

"Mobo's a coke dealer?"

"In a decent world he would be. He was dealing Ritalin, that stuff they give to kids who won't pay attention in school. But he told people it was coke. When you crush it up it's just white powder, and when you snort it it opens up your lungs and gets you real focused on what you're doing, so for these people it was perfect. And none of them would know a bag of coke from a finger up their ass, so they had no idea it wasn't real."

"That's very entrepreneurial of him," I said.

"Yeah, it wasn't a bad idea, I'll give him that. He used to deal at the bowling alley too. Those guys take their league games pretty seriously."

"Yes, they do."

"He even had a plan worked out in case any rival gangs tried to move in, or he thought the feds were on to him. He had copies of all the keys to every apartment in the building. He figured he'd plant the stuff on someone else, let them take the fall."

"I'm just glad he wasn't using my place to take shits."

"What?"

"Nothing."

"Kahuna Karaoke is where he met Marlene Burton, and then

they started up their little affair. They used to come back to his place after they were done for the night. I'm surprised you never heard them. He said she was a screamer."

"The scream of the deaf," I said quietly. "So he wasn't fucking his guinea pig."

"All right, if you're gonna get weird I'll just—"

"No, sorry. It's just, forget it. Please, go on."

He shook his head.

"They went on like that for a while, and then she just stopped showing up. That was the end of it. He hadn't seen her for a few weeks and since he had no way to get in touch with her he figured that was it. He had no idea she was dead. We knew that as soon as we told him, just from the look on his face. This guy wasn't smart enough to fake anything."

"So who killed Marlene?"

"Nobody. Two days ago we got a call from a lady who lives in the house next door to the Burtons, and she was hysterical. Turns out her fourteen-year-old son is a peeping Tom, and he'd been taping Marlene Burton in the shower for months. He had a clear shot of her bathroom mirror from his bedroom window. He was taping the night she died. She slipped as she stepped into the shower and fell backwards and smacked her head on the tile floor. It was an accident, just like we'd figured all along. Her husband confirmed that she was clumsy. The week before she tripped into a door knob and gave herself a black eye."

"Touché," I said. "So the kid showed the tape of her in the shower to his mom?"

"No, she walked in on him masturbating to it. She thought it was one of those German snuff films. She'd just seen a special on CNN about them, so she called us to report him."

"Some people shouldn't be allowed to watch cable," I said. "And she turned in her own son?"

"Yep."

"It figures. These are the days of tyranny and bullshit in which we live."

"You finished?"

"I think so. But if you thought all along that she died accidentally why did you bring me in and make me jerk off into that plastic bag?"

"We have to examine all the possible scenarios," he said. "Detective work is really just the elimination of possibility. You see," he bit his lip, trying to hold it in, then started laughing. "I'm sorry. I'm just fucking around with you," and he kept laughing, and pointing at me. "We figured you hadn't done anything, we were just having some fun. That's the thing. Everybody thinks cops are such hard asses, but most of the time we're just fucking around. Nobody realizes how funny we are."

"That must be really hard for you."

"Don't be mad," he said, sweet talking me like I was an asshole. "Anyway her husband was so sure you'd killed her we had to play along with him for a little while, just to get his mind off things. You have to think of the victim's family in these situations."

"That's true," I said.

"Of course we didn't think he'd try and kill you or anything. We obviously wouldn't have kept it up if we thought that's what he had in mind."

"That means a lot to me."

"So we closed out the Marlene Burton case, but we still had Beekman to deal with, and your landlord. We usually like to stick it to these pharmaceutical-type offenders, just because it's so embarrassing."

"Prescription drug addicts are kind of humiliating."

"Your landlord even started going through withdrawal. We offered to enroll him in a methadone clinic, just kidding around, you know? But he said he didn't want to quit. All he had left was his music, and he needed the Ritalin he thought was coke to perform."

"Just like Huey Lewis in *Duets*."

"He said if doing drugs and singing your heart out was wrong he didn't want to be right."

"I'm the same way about stealing saltshakers."

He looked at me for a minute, and somewhere crickets were chirping.

"Anyway, him and Beekman worked out an arrangement. In exchange for free fake junk your landlord did all the dealing down at Kahuna Karaoke and the bowling alley and he referred big clients to Beekman's apartment. That's who he thought me and Brooks were when we knocked on the door."

"An honest mistake."

"He started a little taxi service for Beekman too, driving Marlene Burton to and from his apartment on Tuesday nights after he was finished dealing. Beekman told us that, not your landlord. We couldn't wait to throw it at him though, just to see how he'd react."

"That does explain things," I said.

"And get this. For an extra baggie a week, he pimped out his wife to him."

"What?"

"Every Thursday night Beekman stopped in on the guy's wife

while he was out singing George Clinton covers cracked out on children's medication."

"Mobo and Bryce's wife?"

"Every Thursday," he said. "That's some sick circle you were running around in down here."

"Why?"

"Why what?"

"Why would she do that?"

"Why does anybody do anything? People are stupid. Maybe she was getting a cut. Maybe she liked the guy. I don't see how, but maybe she did. Maybe she had some kind of retard fetish, who knows. Working this job you learn not to ask why people do the stupid shit they do. You just put as many of them in jail as you can and move on."

"Yeah," I said.

"So then we came down here to find this. What a mess. Your landlord killed himself pretty good. A big fat bullet in the head. Nobody knows where the wife is."

"But I heard two shots."

"Yeah, there were two shots fired. The first one either he was shooting at her or he was shooting at himself. Either way he missed. The second blew out the back of his skull."

"Yuck," I said.

"Yep."

We both looked at the sidewalk. It was a moment of silence.

"So where do you fit into all of this?" he said.

"I'm just not sure about that."

"You have any idea where the wife might've taken off to?"

"Nope."

"Supposedly she was spotted outside the bus station late last night, but that's all we've got. The woman fit the description, but we're still not sure it was her. I doubt she'd even be charged with anything. It looks like your basic case of stupidity and suicide, but we'd like to ask her a few questions anyway."

"I know what you mean."

"We've still got Beekman in a holding cell down at the station. He's trying to plea bargain down to a lesser charge of fireworks possession on the condition we don't tell his parents about the Ritalin. Fireworks possession isn't even a crime in this state," he said, and laughed again. "We're gonna keep him around for a while, see what he comes up with next. The guy's pretty entertaining."

"Yeah," I said.

"We've still got your sperm down in the lab. You want us to just throw it out?"

"Eww. Yeah."

"And what do you want us to do about Brian Burton?"

"Who?'

"Marlene Burton's husband? The guy who tried to gun you down in the street last week? That one is considered a crime in this state. Most states actually. He's still in the hospital but he should be getting out in a few days. You want to press charges?"

"Nah. It was just a misunderstanding. Some bad detective work by him. Anyway he's got no hand."

"That's nice of you," he said.

"Yeah. I'm a nice guy."

The one message on my answering machine was from Gwen. She'd left it on Friday at 4:57 P.M. She sounded kind of sarcastic:

"Hello *Shane*? It's Gwendolyn. I hope you're enjoying your soon-to-be permanent unemployment. See, I had a little talk with my friends in HR and I told them *all* about you. Then they had a talk with *their* friends, and then *they* talked to *their* friends. It was quite an email chain we made. Don't bother even *thinking* about applying for a job at Panopticon, or any of its subsidiaries. Or any other insurance company in the *state* for that matter. If you even *try* to pick up an application you'll be led out of the building by security. Best of luck though finding a new *career*. Your *ass* is *grass*."

Just before she hung up, right as the phone hit the cradle, I heard a woman's voice go "Woo—" The beginning of all her co-workers and friends saying, "Woooo! You *go* girl! I can't believe you *did* that! Oh my *god!* That was *awesome!*" Then there were high fives. There was clapping. Someone said, "Girl power!" Maybe one of the guys said, "Wow. I never want to get on *your* bad side! Har har," and then had a secret crush on her because she was so strong and tough, and with her for a girlfriend maybe he'd finally, finally be able to stand up to his mother.

I hoped so. That was just about what she deserved. She really did. And she deserved the satisfaction of that phone call. I was going to let her have it. For a few months anyway, until she'd forgotten all about me. Until she came into work one Monday morning to me on her voice mail, telling her in a quiet, somber voice that my test results had just come back positive and I had full-blown AIDS. I'd pause dramatically to control my emotions and laugh into my hand as I held the phone away. I'd apologize and beg her to get tested as soon as she could, and to keep getting tested for at least a year, just to make sure, and to contact all of her other recent partners and tell them to do the same. I'd say,

"May the Lord Jesus Christ bring you comfort and peace in these difficult times Gwendolyn." I'd tell her she was in my prayers. Then I'd hang up.

Maybe I wouldn't, but maybe I would. Her attempt to spite me was so misguided I felt like I almost had to. Two wrongs don't make a right but sometimes they make me laugh. I am a vengeful god.

The day I left I took the M-80 I'd gotten from Mobo before he was Rick Beekman and I blew the shit out of my tiny bike helmet. Vulcanized rubber shrapnel pelted the side of my building and rained down on me like a baptism as I ducked behind a Dumpster. And it was good.

I was going to put the sparkler on Marlene's grave, but I didn't know where she was buried and I'd already forgotten what her last name was, so that didn't work out. I lit it anyway and stood there like the Statue of Liberty as it flared in my hand, the remains of my bike helmet scattered around me like the ashes of a life I would never admit to leading. I did it for Marlene, and for America. And for me too.

The sky was gray and it looked like it would rain. I hoped that it would. I like to leave places in the rain. It gives things a poignancy that has absolutely nothing to do with me.

I walked down the street with my bag over my shoulder and looked around, finally trying to notice all the things about the city that I'd missed all these months, knowing that I wouldn't remember any of it anyway. Whenever I'm leaving I get sentimental for that nostalgia I know I won't have the next day.

I stood at an intersection and looked up at an abandoned

building that could have belonged to any city in America, but I tried to fix it on that street corner at that time of day, and remember it there and nowhere else. It was around three o'clock and nothing special was happening, but I tried not to forget it anyway. And as I struggled to create some scenic memories of my time there in my own doomed, after-the-fact sort of way, the General Lee pulled up beside me.

I dropped my bag and stood with my mouth hanging open in the wind. It was idling at the red light. From that angle it couldn't possibly run me over. I had to know. I walked over and tried to look through the glass but I couldn't see past the tinting. So I knocked. I heard the hum of the electric window as it slowly, slowly unrolled. And there was Karal, sitting in the driver's seat.

He was slouched over with his head bowed, his chin pressed into his chest. His hands were both up over his head, gripping two triangle bars that were connected to the steering wheel by an elaborate set of wires and pulleys. His legs were spread wide, his right foot jammed all the way over on the passenger side, and there was a huge pedal hooked under each of his shoes like they were ski boots snapped into bindings.

I stood at the window staring at this puppet show, and Karal swung his head over to look at me. Then he gave me the biggest grin in the world. He was thrilled to see me. I had no idea what to do. Karal smacked his head into the middle of the steering wheel and the horn groaned "Dixie."

Then the light turned green and he slammed both his feet down and swung his arms like he was conducting an orchestra at some wild, fantastic finale. He gunned the engine and nearly ran down an old woman who hadn't made it all the way through the crosswalk. There was a handicapped sticker on his license plate, so that made everything okay. And the General Lee took off, swerving all over the street.

I walked down to the waterfront, back to the Japanese memorial where Marlene had called me Stink for the last time. I hadn't met any Japanese people while I was in town, but I'd decided to remember them anyway.

The park was empty and the river had gone gray, reflecting the overcast sky in its dirty ripples. It was getting colder. I put my collar up against the wind and on a copper plaque laid into a four-foot-tall Stonehenge rock I read an excerpt of a speech by Ronald Reagan:

> *The sad chapter in our history . . . teaches an invaluable lesson: that our Constitution is based on a belief in the innate, God-given worth of every individual, and that this worth cannot be denied without diminishing and endangering us all.*

I walked away and stood on the paved concrete path, leaning my elbows on the wrought-iron railing, and I looked out across the gray water at the spirals of highway on the other side and the long bridges stretching towards them.

I should have heard a baby crying somewhere, or an ambulance siren wailing as it raced down the street behind me. I should have seen a homeless man sleeping under a newspaper or a junkie passed out grinding his teeth and gripping his scarred, pot-holed arm. Preferably a junkie who was Japanese, or at least Asian. That would have been perfect. That would have been right.

Instead I heard the saxophone of an unseen street musician from further down the walking path. He was playing "Careless Whisper" by George Michael. And then I saw Doug coming towards me.

He was wearing tan leggings bunched up around his knees and a white wraparound tunic with a thick white belt high on his waist. He looked like he was on his way to a *Star Wars* convention. Like fucking Luke Skywalker, and the years since *Return of the Jedi* had not been kind. His right arm was in a sling, and he was wearing an orange headband. Before I could throw myself into the river and drown he'd seen me.

"Shane!" He waved his free left arm and galloped towards me like the damaged, awkward, middle-aged man that he was.

"Hey!" he said gasping, totally out of breath. His strawberry blond curls hung over his headband and dripped sweat down his face. It drained into his ragged mustache and was lost. He had sprinted almost six yards. "Long time no see!"

"Hi Doug."

"Wow, it's been a while."

"Yeah. What happened to your arm? The bus?"

"No, I don't ride the bus anymore. I tore my rotator cuff trying to open a banana."

"Christ Doug."

"It was really unripe. I was yanking on the stem and then *rip!*" He winced at the memory as he touched his good hand to his bad shoulder. "I had to have Tommy John surgery. That's what the doctor called it. He was an athlete I think. I'm on my way to rehab now. I learned my lesson though. You should always cut your bananas open, even if they look yellow enough to break. Believe me. I found out the hard way."

"I didn't know there was a hard way to open a banana."

"Neither did I," and he shook his head. "But I'm really doing great. My episodes are almost gone! I don't even carry my iced tea flask around anymore. Remember? DWI? Ha ha ha ha."

"Yeah," I said.

"I haven't ridden the bus in weeks. I bought a scooter."

"Honda?"

"No, Huffy. It's the kind you stand on and kick off with your leg. The one all the kids have. It's hard going up hills, and I can't ride with my arm like this, but it's much healthier than the bus. It's good cardiovascular, and it's much safer for your noggin, ha ha ha."

"Jesus Doug."

"Ahhh . . . so I guess you heard about Marlene?"

"Yeah."

"That was such a shame. Such a shame," he said, and looked down at his feet. "The police called me in for questioning. And tests. She and I had a sexual relationship you know."

The dirty water beckoned to me from below.

"It wasn't right, but it happened. I miss her." And he looked out over the river. "Her death really made me look at my own life. That's when I decided to make some changes. I stopped riding the bus and bought my scooter. I eat a lot more vegetables now too."

"That's nice," I said.

"I'm still looking for a new permanent assistant. Right now I have a temp. Davinder. He's from India. He goes by Davey. Very smart, and he can hear too. You don't know him. You missed your last appointment actually. I tried calling you but—"

"Yeah, where are you headed again? Rehab? Is that your, uh, uniform?"

"I suppose it is. The doctor said I needed to do something that would work a full range of motion, give me more flexibility to help my tendons heal, so I started taking yoga. Don't worry, it's not some hippie New Age thing. I'm in a class with Yogi Finkelstein. He teaches a much more non-traditional, non-denominational type of rabbinical yoga, and he brings in French philosophy and pagan fertility rituals and all kinds of neat things."

"Sounds like a liberal arts degree."

"You know, it really is," he said reflectively. "It's supposed to be performed in a natural hot spring wading pool, but there aren't any around so we go to the Y."

"That's fantastic. Listen, I've got to take off. I have to catch a bus."

"Oh you're leaving town? I wondered what the bag was for."

"Yeah, it's my time."

"Oh, okay. Well, best of luck to you Shane. It was great having you as a patient. If you're ever in town again stop by the office. I still keep a pitcher of iced tea handy, just in case, ha ha."

"Okay."

"And take care of your teeth. You're going to need some foundational work eventually. Those spot repairs I did aren't going to hold up forever. You really shouldn't go too long without seeing a professional. Remember, ignore your teeth and they'll go away, ha ha ha."

"Ha ha ha," I said as I was backing away from him.

"And watch your head getting off that bus!"

"Yeah."

"Oh, and about those outstanding bills you have."

Shit.

"You're not going to pay them, are you."

"Probably not Doug."

"That's what I thought," he said, but he was smiling, like only a man who's wearing an orange headband on his way to see Yogi Finkelstein possibly could. He looked ridiculously serene and at peace with the world and with me, both of whom were obviously screwing him.

"That's okay. We had some laughs, didn't we?"

"Sure Doug."

"Yeah, we did." And he put his free hand on his hip and sighed, quietly reminiscing. "All right, hurry up and don't miss your bus. And wherever you go, find yourself a yogi when you get there. It really helps."

"Okay," I said.

He walked along the water and whistled the tune to "Splish Splash I Was Taking a Bath," snapping his fingers as he went, which mingled with the saxophone solo from "Careless Whisper" that was blowing up the concrete path to meet him. And this soundtrack somehow described Dr. Douglas Weinhardt more completely than words ever could. Guilty feet have got no rhythm. Rub a dub Doug. Rub a dub.

I was on my way to the bus station. Despite everything I felt pretty good. I wasn't skipping down the sidewalk or anything, but I liked some things about myself and I didn't want to die. It was the closest I'd been to optimistic in years.

And I was rich, which always helps, no matter what rich people say. I still had some money left from those paychecks Panopticon Insurance had given me for sleeping in their bathroom, and I'd saved a lot from not paying rent the past few months. And I had a check, made out to me, for $800 in my back pocket. Marlene's husband had been in the hospital since that night he'd tried to murder me, and with no hand and so much else on his mind I doubt he would've thought to call his bank to cancel a check. There were a few flecks of dried blood on Marvin the Martian's face, but there's always a check cashing window that doesn't care about those kinds of details. And it's always by the bus station, no matter what city you're in.

I was still a little torn up about Bryce's wife, and when that detective told me about her and Mobo, that finally broke my heart actually. So maybe I really wasn't feeling all that fucking optimistic. Maybe I was pretty fucking sad. Even so, I was still hoping I'd run into her somehow, and I thought for some reason that I would. I wanted to see her again, and ask her a few questions maybe, and that was something. It wasn't enough, but it was something.

At least I had some things to think about.

So I walked towards the station and I waited for it to rain. And it did, which was nice.